GOOD TWIN, BAD TWIN
MICHAEL J PECK

GOOD TWIN
BAD TWIN

MICHAEL J PECK

Good Twin, Bad Twin

PROLOGUE

Ethan was moving but not of his own accord. It was a confusing and involuntary action as his senses were dulled and his mind was spinning. He couldn't make sense of where he was or what was happening, the darkness around him alienating him further. He tried to cry out, but barely a breath was forced from his terror-constricted throat, and his limbs strived to shake with fear but instead lay limp and useless. He was aware now of strong hands holding him, many hands, turning him, forcing him away from the safety of his room, taking him to who knows where while he offered no resistance. Why couldn't he fight back? He couldn't think clearly and felt liquid running from his mouth, drooling down his chin as his eyes rolled to the back of his head. He felt nauseous, his stomach seemingly travelling ahead of him while the rest of him languished in a flaccid state.

He sucked in a lungful of air, trying to add sustenance to his deprived brain, furtively attempting to focus his thoughts, but could only muster enough concentration to ask himself one fleeting question: was he drugged? It didn't make sense, nothing made sense; he wasn't even sure if it was real.

He felt pain in his legs, dropped onto something hard. They were then lifted and floating again, pulling him further onwards to an unknown destination. He heard someone speak but the sounds were muffled, drawn out as though in slow motion. Above him stars appeared, or were they lights? Whatever they were, they made his head spin uncontrollably and he knew he was about to pass out. As more indistinguishable words floated around his head, a sudden, horror-stricken thought gripped him, a memory that had been so repressed he had convinced himself it wasn't real. But as his final few seconds of consciousness graced him, he knew without a doubt that this had happened before.

CHAPTER 1

The world was returning. Light filtered down into his bloodshot eyes which were slowly opening, attempting to focus. The brightness encompassed him, forcing him to painfully blink as his lids worked against the dryness. He gave a cry in panic and tried to swallow, but his coarse throat made him cough uncontrollably. Gulping in air, he struggled to sit upright, pulling himself up with exaggerated effort and gasped, but his sense of panic began subsiding as he took in his surroundings.

He was on a bed, which was soft underneath him. Cozy red sheets draped across his legs. He was in a small room, with a transparent plastic bedside drawer beside him and a curtain pulled out across the length of the bed to obscure his vision as to what may have been on the other side. In front of the bed was a door, closed, with no sign of any handle. Bright light emanated throughout the room, apparently originating from the ceiling but with no obvious sign of exactly where it was coming from. The light had a purple hue to it, bathing him in comforting warmth.

Ethan lifted his arms, checking they moved, and noticed his clothes. He was wearing a casual black jacket, cream top and dark green pants. His socks were black with patterns of birds printed on them. Interesting, he thought. He didn't recognise his clothes, but it didn't go against what he may have chosen for himself. He moved his head and felt pain streak up from the back of his neck to the top of his skull. Reaching up he became aware of a constriction around his neck. It felt like a collar but it was stuck cohesively to his skin. He tried moving it, but it didn't budge. *What the…?* He tugged harder, but it was stuck fast. He had no idea why something would be placed around his neck, but the thought of it gave him feelings of suffocation. He gasped as though it were indeed choking him, but then remonstrated with himself that it wasn't, it was just uncomfortable. Clearly, he wasn't going to get it off, so with some self-control he decided to deal with it later. His first priority was to find out where he was and if he was safe.

Slowly he moved his legs over to the edge of the bed, allowing them to fall and checking that they, too, were not injured. A pain throbbed in the back of his calf, and on inspection a purple bruise glared up at him. He tried to remember how he got it, but his mind was still unfocussed and confused.

What the hell was going on? How did he get here, wherever 'here' was? His thoughts began churning, and a host of other uncomfortable questions bombarded their way into his consciousness. What happened yesterday, or a week ago? Where did he come from? He couldn't actually remember what he did, where he lived or who were his friends and family. In fact, he had no recollection of ever having talked to another person. He shook his head as though somehow it would help to clear any imaginary blockages. Panic began rising in him again as he realised that something was very wrong. There was absolutely nothing he could cling onto; his past was an empty shell. He had completely lost his memory.

In his panicked state, Ethan jumped up off the bed in alarm as the door suddenly slid open. What he saw next did nothing to ease his tension. A bird flew in; or more exactly, a bird that actually looked like a robotic parrot. Its body was metallic and coloured in various hues of red, blue, yellow and orange. It hovered excitedly in front of him.

'Patient five is awake. Patient five is awake,' it exclaimed, its metallic wings moving so fast they were almost impossible to see.

Ethan retreated from the creature to the wall behind. He noted its gleaming red beak and wondered if it was going to attack him. He opened his mouth to verbalise his surprise, however the bird interrupted him, apparently anticipating his next words.

'Please do not swear. It contravenes article twelve and is, quite frankly, vulgar. Please reconsider your next declaration.'

Ethan didn't know what to say as he continued to stare, but could only come out with an obvious statement.

'You're a talking robot parrot.'

The parrot seemed to become agitated, the buzzing noise it omitted becoming higher in pitch.

'So?' it retorted, apparently offended. 'There's nothing unusual about that. Talking parrots have been the rage for many years *despite* what you may have heard!'

Ethan shook his head, faltering. 'I haven't heard anything at all.' He found himself speaking in an apologetic tone and slightly defensive. 'I don't even know what you are.' He looked almost pleadingly at the creature. 'What are you?'

This seemed to get the bird even more offended.

'What am I? What? I am not a what! I am a sophisticated, type six, fully integrated, programmed and trained security person with personality map over-driving. I am a functioning being like yourself!'

Ethan was taken aback. 'Okay. Um… do you have a name?'

'Of course!' the bird retorted.

There was silence as Ethan waited. 'Well, what is it then?' he eventually asked.

The bird seemed to hesitate. 'Budgie.'

Despite himself, Ethan smirked slightly. 'Budgie? But you're a parrot.'

The bird made a noise which sounded much like a sigh. 'My creator didn't know a lot about birds,' he seemed to confess, 'which is surprising, all things considered!'

Ethan had to smile at the absurd creature. 'Why was it surprising?' he asked.

'Because my creator likes flora and fauna.' Budgie gave a cough, as though preparing for a speech. 'My creator revolutionised security, ensuring that the different persuasions live in perfect harmony to enable a stable and peaceful civilisation.'

Ethan couldn't help but think it was a well-used and programmed statement. But what he said held his interest.

'Different persuasions? What do you mean by that?'

Budgie zoomed in closer to Ethan. The bird's eyes came out on stalks and spun around in circles, inspecting him closely. Ethan took a side-ways step.

'You are damaged?'

Ethan had to admit that he probably was. 'I can't remember anything. I seem to have lost my memory.'

Budgie said logically, 'That would explain why you are in a hospital. The clues fit.'

Ethan acknowledged the bird's amazing deduction with a nod, thankful that at least he now knew where he was, and presumably safe.

'So, who are the different persuasions?'

Budgie paused before replying. 'I would encourage you to exercise some logical thought on the matter, get your neurotransmitters transmitting. It may help speed up your recovery.'

Ethan felt annoyed. 'Can't you just tell me? I don't remember anything!'

'It is for your own good. I am putting your health above my own desire to tell you. And please don't forget to say thank you.'

With that, the bird spun around and flew out the door, almost colliding with the man who was walking in.

Shaking his head in disbelief at the automaton's logic, Ethan's attention turned to the man. The first thing he noted was the collar around his neck. It was grey, about five centimetres in width and fitted very snugly above the top of his shoulders. Ethan's hand went automatically to his own collar and knew it must be identical. The rest of the man's clothes looked like a uniform and it quickly occurred to Ethan he was a nurse, though he had no recollection of when he may have actually seen a nurse before. The uniform itself was white, apart from broad lapels which were light blue with matching cuffs and breast pocket. It gave an officious and slightly geeky appearance, which seemed to agree with the general disposition of the man wearing it. His rounded glasses and plastered down black hair completed the effect.

'Hello there,' he said kindly, although hurriedly. 'Very nice to see you awake at last.' Ethan opened his mouth to speak but the man continued talking.

'I hope Budgie has not been too difficult; he can be a bit temperamental and get too involved with the patients. My name's Sebastian and I'm your nurse for today.' He gave a small fake laugh. 'Well, I will be if I can have some time to be.' He pushed away some hair which had fallen across one eye. 'There are far too many patients. Too many, and they keep coming.' He emphasised the word 'coming' and gave a rather rancid laugh. 'But that's not your problem; I'm sure you have other issues to worry about, like getting better.' He drew out a device from his top pocket which resembled a torch in size and shape and pointed it towards Ethan.

'What's that?' Ethan said nervously.

Sebastian ignored Ethan's question, and instead was looking at the device intently before shaking it, and then gave a bashful smile. 'I better turn it on I suppose, it should work better that way.' He turned it around to fiddle with a switch before it suddenly came to life and enveloped him with a yellow light. He seemed to be taken by surprise and switched it off again, which gave Ethan a moment to speak.

'Can you tell me what's going on? What's wrong with me?'

The nurse sighed and looked forlorn.

'Well, if we knew that we would fix you up and send you home. The doctors here are very good, so give them time and they'll sort you out. Do you remember anything about how you got here?'

Ethan struggled to reach back into his thoughts, searching for some remnant of memory or clue. He wasn't sure if his desperation to remember actually hindered his attempt, but it became quickly clear to him that there was nothing he could hold on to; nothing at all.

'No,' he exhaled, his voice cracking slightly. 'I… I remember my name, it's Ethan, but…' He shook his head. 'There's nothing else.' Ethan's heart sank as he heard the words come from his own mouth. He looked up at the nurse. 'Do *you* know how I got here?'

The nurse patted him on the shoulder and sat down on the bed next to him. 'All I know is that the human security force found you. Or rather rescued you from whoever was kidnapping you. You were unconscious, and they brought you back here this morning. We did some tests on you, but nothing has come back so far as to why you were not conscious; possibly you were given some kind of drug or potion. It's all very mysterious.'

Ethan tried to digest this small bit of information, not completely understanding. 'Why would I be kidnapped?'

Sebastian held his hands up in bewilderment.

'No idea. Maybe you did something bad. Do you think you would've?'

Before he had a chance to answer, the door slid

open and Budgie flew in, almost skidding to a rapid halt mid-air.

'Unacceptable questioning! Desist this line of conversation!'

Sebastian looked both affronted and annoyed.

'You shouldn't listen in on a private, nurse to patient conversation.'

It was Budgie's turn to sound affronted.

'Well, you shouldn't be asking him questions like that. I've got better things to do than monitor for illegal bantering!'

Sebastian raised an eyebrow. 'Really, are you sure?' he muttered, standing up from the bed. 'Because all I see you do is fly around bothering people.'

Budgie's eyes turned a violent shade of red and grew suddenly larger.

'I am an essential part of the techno-security operation in this establishment. Some respect would be advised. I do have offensive abilities.'

Sebastian held up his hands as though defeated.

'Okay, okay. I'm impressed. No need to get all flappy.'

Ethan smirked. 'What did he say wrong anyway?' he asked Budgie curiously.

The parrot seemed to shake its head and its clawed feet spun around in circles on its metal joints. 'Unbelievable audacity! He asked you if you were *bad*!'

It was Sebastian's turn to shake his head. 'No, I didn't. I asked him if he did something bad, that's different.'

'It amounts to the same thing,' Budgie protested

and turned to leave, but not before finishing with, 'And may your twin be with you always.' He flew out the door.

Sebastian smiled. 'He says that, so he seems more human. It's kind of cute.'

Ethan was totally lost as to what just happened or the meaning of their conversation, and this was clearly written all over his face.

Sebastian opened his mouth to speak but the cuffs on his jacket suddenly started flashing as though there were hidden lights inside. He touched one cuff and the flashing stopped.

'Looks like I'm needed elsewhere. I'll come back later and explain some things to you.'

As he turned to leave, a deep voice came out from behind the curtain that was next to Ethan's bed.

'Don't worry. I can talk to him, I'm bored anyway.'

Sebastian snapped his fingers and said, 'Retract,' and the curtain vanished into thin air. Ethan stared unbelievingly.

'Where did the curtain go?' he asked.

Sebastian smiled. 'Well, it was never really there,' he said, as though that explained everything.

Ethan's confusion about the curtain was short-lived as his attention was diverted to the patient who had been revealed behind it. It was a boy of around Ethan's age, perhaps seventeen or eighteen, who was also on a bed with another curtain to his right.

'Okay, well you two can get to know each other,' Sebastian said. 'And I'll keep going.'

Sebastian left, leaving Ethan to survey his

roommate somewhat tentatively. The first thing he noticed was that the boy wore white. White trousers which matched white shoes and a tight-fitting, white tunic top. The boy's black hair was in contrast and swept backwards from his forehead, giving him a somewhat ostentatious look. The boy also had a collar around his neck similar to Sebastian's, and his fingers on both hands were covered in rings of various sizes and materials. He was looking at Ethan with a penetrative stare which Ethan was having trouble interpreting. It took him a few seconds before he settled on how it made him feel and he felt a slight shudder across his shoulders. The boy made Ethan feel cold.

'I'm Mistix,' he drawled, the corners of his mouth sloping upwards into a faint smile. 'You're looking a bit lost.'

It took Ethan a few seconds before he replied.

'That would be an understatement,' he said simply.

The other boy nodded, apparently understanding completely.

'You don't remember anything?'

Ethan shook his head, slightly annoyed that he had to say once more that he remembered nothing.

Looking suitably sympathetic, the corners of Mistix's mouth turned down slightly as though sad. Yet somehow, Ethan didn't believe his empathy.

'Maybe I can help you,' the newcomer offered. The tone of his voice was somewhat deadpan and seemed more like a statement than an extension of a friendly act. Nevertheless, Ethan was not going to refuse.

'I've got a hundred questions.' It sounded like an apology.

The other boy shrugged. 'I've got the time, not much to do in hospital anyway.'

This was all the encouragement Ethan needed, and his mind flooded with thoughts. 'Where did the curtain go?' he asked with some amazement.

Laughing, Mistix obviously thought the question was insignificant.

'It was just a hologram, all the curtains around us are. They can keep patients' privacy without having to touch anything, easier to keep everything sterile and *clean*.' He emphasised the word clean as though it were somehow distasteful.

Ethan nodded, satisfied. 'Okay. So… what did Budgie mean when he said something about a twin?'

Turning his head to one side, Mistix looked at Ethan as though disbelieving what he had just asked. 'It's what we all say, of course.'

Ethan was none the wiser. 'Why?'

His roommate frowned. 'You really don't know?' He spoke as though it was absurd that he didn't know. Ethan felt frustration building inside him.

'I don't remember anything. I told you.' Again, he had to say this.

The other boy smirked and looked deep into Ethan as though the answers were there to be found. 'Why don't you remember?' he said slowly.

His gaze didn't abate until Ethan squirmed slightly, becoming obviously uncomfortable. What was it about this guy? He was so intense.

Mistix pulled back and then spoke, matter-of-fact.

'We say it, because it's a quaint way of reminding ourselves how lucky we are to have a twin, even though we may be… different.'

Ethan still didn't understand. 'You and Sebastian have a twin?'

The other boy shook his head as though addressing a simpleton.

'We all have twins. *You* must have a twin.'

Ethan's eyes opened in surprise at this thought. 'Would I? I don't remember.' With some self-admonishment, Ethan mentally kicked himself as now he was voluntarily saying that he did not remember. But could he dare believe that he *did* have a twin?

Mistix sniffed and turned to one side. 'Unless he died, of course.'

Another voice spoke, and a figure strode into the room. 'Fortunately, yours is still alive.'

It took Ethan only a second to realise he was seeing double. The newcomer was the spitting image of Mistix, but unlike Mistix this person was clothed completely in black. In fact, it appeared to be the same outfit as Mistix apart from the colour. The brothers looked the absolute opposite of each other.

'I'm Kredax,' the newcomer introduced, and turned to face his brother.

'I didn't get you any food, the lunch lady is coming. How are you feeling?'

His brother shrugged. 'Like I had a big night out in a Snake-shift bar. I'm fine.'

Kredax studied him. 'Getting blasted by a security automaton is not insignificant. You could have internal injuries.'

Smirking, Mistix was obviously not particularly worried. 'We'll see.'

Kredax continued, while Ethan listened with interest. 'What were you doing, anyway?' He seemed to ask the question cautiously, although with some determination.

'Mistaken identity; wrong place at the wrong time. The birds are developing faults. It's not safe to go outside.'

Kredax looked doubtful. 'There have been rumours about faults in some units. It's not likely though, considering the possible *consequences*.'

Mistix averted his eyes. 'Don't hold on too tight, brother,' he reprimanded.

'It benefits us both.' Kredax spoke like a parent explaining something to a child for the umpteenth time. Mistix's reply was not like that of a child.

'In *your* mind.' There was bitterness in his voice. Ethan sensed he was intruding on a long-discussed topic that he was not privy to.

Kredax seemed to want to change the topic and looked at Ethan. 'Why are you here?' He was direct but not unfriendly.

'I don't really know,' Ethan replied.

'He's lost his memory,' Mistix explained.

Kredax frowned. 'And your twin?'

Ethan shrugged. 'I don't even know if I have one.'

Kredax raised an eyebrow, as though the statement was absurd. 'Weird! Is there anything you can remember?'

Sounding unsure, Ethan looked downtrodden.

'All I know is that I've got bruises on my legs and this thing around my neck…' he indicated the collar, 'but no idea how I got them.'

Kredax looked slightly confused. 'But everyone is given a collar once they turn five years old. You have forgotten that?'

Ethan was perplexed. 'I'm sure I've never had it on before.' Even as he said the words, he realised he had said them far more confidently than he felt.

'How do you know if you can't remember?' Mistix pointed out.

Ethan felt defensive. 'It just doesn't feel right. Why would I have it? What's it for?'

The brothers looked at each other.

'To cover the sign of the heart, of course,' Kredax said.

Ethan was getting tired of sentences which were meant to explain everything but told him nothing.

'I don't know what that means!' he said abruptly, exasperated. 'Can you start from the start? Why are there so many twins and what does the sign of the heart do?'

Looking intrigued, Kredax sat down on the end of his brother's bed.

'If you really can't remember, I'll tell you.' He took a breath before continuing. 'I studied it for my science thesis at school,' he explained. 'So, years ago, our genes were altered due to a disease eradication program. It was a new technology called Antithesis Inoculation, and involved injecting cells into the body which had the ability to change their shape and function. It was really clever stuff at the time. These cells seek out any diseased cells, mirror their structure on it, bind to it and effectively neutralise it.' Kredax made hand movements as though one hand was attacking the other. 'It was like a good cell counteracting its twin bad cell. The program was very successful in immunising against many diseases, but it also unknowingly affected the population's fertility.' He paced up and down, obviously well versed on the subject. 'From that time onward, almost everybody born was a twin, with only very rare incidences of single births.' He paused and glanced sideways at Mistix, before continuing. 'It also had the effect of…' he seemed to try to choose his words carefully, 'altering the neurons in the brain of each twin. It meant each individual had… different outlooks on life, different personalities.'

Mistix laughed scornfully. 'What he means is that one twin is born good and one twin is born bad! Two identities who are so alike, but so opposite to each other; a symbiotic relationship that has to be endured. Forever.' He folded his arms with a sense of finality.

His brother looked down-trodden and calmly added, 'The bond between twins is absolute. Two people who in many ways are one. They cannot live without the other; not easily anyway.'

Ethan studied the twins in front of him, Mistix wearing white, Kredax wearing black, and the comparison was confusing. 'So...are you good?' He was looking at Mistix.

Kredax suddenly looked panicked and gripped Ethan by the shoulders, causing Ethan to stiffen in surprise.

'You can't ask that! It's not allowed!' He looked nervously at the door to the room.

Mistix looked amused at Kredax's reaction.

'Relax. Budgie has probably gone off to bother someone else.' His attention turned to Ethan. 'Am I good? Because I wear white? That's very presumptuous. We wear these colours because we don't like to be stereotyped. Not that I really care anyway if people know. I am who I am!' He got off his bed and walked up to Ethan. 'But if you are really interested, and really want to know.' His eyes were level with Ethan's, staring into him with a subtle glint which seemed enhanced by the vague purple hue of the room. 'I'm the bad one!'

Ethan knew what Mistix was going to say before he said it, but nevertheless the chills that arced across his shoulders forced him to lean backwards as much as he could, trapped by the fact that he was still sitting on the bed. Kredax stepped forward and gently eased Mistix back.

'It's okay,' Kredax reassured. 'He's not as extreme as he makes out. We're just different.'

Looking from one to the other, Ethan asked, 'And what about these collars? What do they do?'

Mistix blurted out, 'It hides who we really are! Underneath each collar is a permanent mark on the back of your neck; a heart that's right side up if you're good or a heart upside down if you're bad. They're burnt into your skin when you're five years old, an age where people will know you well enough to determine what kind of heart you get to keep for the rest of your life; a label to be checked in case they need to know exactly where you stand.'

Reaching for his own collar, Ethan exclaimed, 'But I've never had this on me before! I would... remember.' His voice trailed off as he realised how stupid it sounded under the circumstances.

'Everybody has one,' Mistix affirmed. 'No exceptions.'

'According to who?' Ethan demanded.

It was Kredax who answered. 'The Society of Technology and Potions. The organisation that maintains unity within our people. With such a polarised population it would be impossible to exist together without a regulatory authority.'

'They are, of course, fine examples of the *good* people in our city,' Mistix explained drily.

Ethan tugged at his collar. 'How do we get them off?'

'You can't,' Mistix drawled. 'They are bio-coded and can only be opened by a member of the Society associated with the security forces. So, like us, you are stuck with it.'

Ethan looked determined. 'We'll see,' he said obstinately.

Outside, darkness had crept in, encircling the massive structure of the hospital, a monolith against a starless sky. The streets were tight, an interwoven network of pathways crammed in against each other, buildings seemingly leaning over the next, competing in stature and brightness. It was a city of unequalled technology, but also unequalled division. People went about their business, subtly glancing at others going by, watching them out of the corner of their eye until safely passed, some comforted by the buzz of a hovering bird on surveillance above.

Voices floated in the air from a side alley, excitable and playful, the product of a few too many ciders at the local Snake-shift bar. Two young men were leaning on each other as they staggered down the road, laughing raucously and without regard to anyone who might have minded their bantering. Their clothes were dishevelled and stained, covered with some of the beverages they had consumed that evening.

'You were amazing, Anton!' the man on the left shouted, messing his companion's hair in congratulations. 'I thought you were gone. I can't believe you got out of it!'

Anton laughingly agreed, apparently astounded by his own abilities.

'*I* wasn't sure there for a second. When it turned into the snake, it was way bigger than I thought.'

'I was going to throw a potion at you to get you out.'

'No way, Esiah!' Anton shouted excitedly. 'You do that, and it breaks the rules, you don't get the free booze and *that's* what we're there for!' Both laughed in agreement and veered sideways across the road, before coming to an abrupt halt as the momentum waned and they veered back once more.

'Anyway,' Anton continued. 'Next time it's your turn and you better make sure we get the good stuff. I don't want to be sucking on rodent juice; I want the top shelf, the distilled blood of the hounded beast!'

'That's too good for you, brother,' Esiah teased. 'One sip of that and the Snake-shift would have you beaten before it even transformed from a bunny bear!'

'Well, you better start with a warmed-up mantle milk to get some courage! Or get some tips from your brave older brother.'

Esiah slapped him energetically on the back. 'I can't argue with that after what I saw tonight. Best one I've seen and the biggest snake as well!'

He stopped walking and reached into his coat pocket, pulling out a green bottle, half full of liquid. A security bird appeared from around a nearby corner and moved in closer to them. Neither of the young men noticed. Or if they did, it was barely of any interest to their intoxicated minds. Besides, the birds were everywhere; people were so used to them that they hardly registered in people's consciousness. Esiah raised the bottle in salute to his brother.

'To another great night out; may there be many more!' He took a deep swig from the bottle, gulping greedily before handing it to Anton. His brother also drank recklessly, spilling some down his front and dripping onto the ground below. Both boys laughed and staggered a little more. The bird moved in closer, hovering just above them, noting their movements and environment. Its sensors swept the area, registering no other life forms in the immediate proximity and the secluded section of the alleyway. Anton looked up and saw the bird for the first time and grinned cheekily, raising his bottle in salute.

'Hey, birdy!' he chirped happily. 'Come join the party! Have a drink on us!'

The bird faced him, its electronic wings humming slightly as it maintained a single spot in the air.

'Come on down!' Anton encouraged. 'Stick your beak in this.'

He waved the bottle encouragingly, as though somehow this would tempt the bird to try some. The bird didn't move; instead, it just stared, its electronic pupils dilating.

'Don't just fly there like a stunned Changeling. Join us!' Anton grinned up at it like it was an old friend, expecting participation.

The bird still didn't react, and in fact, gave no response whatsoever. Anton's grin wavered, as it became obvious he was not going to get the reaction he expected. The silence was unusual as the birds would always respond when spoken to. Esiah took hold of his arm, slightly unnerved by the lack of interaction from the automaton.

'Come on,' he encouraged, pulling Anton slightly. 'This one's not in the party mood.'

Anton looked disappointed, lowering his raised arm.

'You're boring!' he insulted and sulkily took a few steps. The bird followed him, still silent, but apparently focused on the young men. Anton's playfulness was quickly changing. 'Well, don't go following us feather-beak. We're too much fun for you.'

They started moving purposefully away from it, but it continued to maintain a distance of only a few metres behind them.

'What's wrong with you?' Esiah snapped, aware that the creature was behaving abnormally. 'Say something or go away. We're not doing anything wrong.'

Despite his protestation, the bird still followed. They cast anxious looks over their shoulders, watching as its eyes suddenly grew larger and larger and extended out onto stalks. Both men became instinctively nervous despite their drunkenness. Turning to walk faster, they failed to notice the eyes change to a violent shade of red; they were angry and burning. Its body quivered slightly, before unleashing a torrent of unbridled heat. It blasted the two men off their feet, sending them catapulting through the air.

Their smoking bodies hit the ground, abruptly extinguishing a night of frivolity and replacing it with unexpected carnage. The bird hovered above its devastation for only a few seconds more before turning and flying off into the distance.

From the shadows behind, a new figure stirred, having watched the last few moments of the altercation. As she moved, a slight sliver of light played across her face, highlighting her sunken appearance and cloaked head, displaying her emotionless features. The Nun did not react to the scene in front of her, but rather slipped back to where she came from.

CHAPTER 2

The conversation in the hospital room was interrupted as the door opened and in walked an elderly lady with an astounding creature, which Ethan could only describe as a cross between a jellyfish and octopus. He wasn't sure if he should be afraid of this thing, but the twins next to him gave no reaction. It was scuttling along on six tentacle-like legs about waist height with an opaque body. Two beady eyes stared unblinkingly forwards. On top of the creature sat a tray with various, square, black objects sitting upon it. Ethan felt revolted, and he couldn't understand why such a thing would be inside a hospital.

The lady leaned over her obtrusive companion, her long grey hair swaying as she moved, her eyes peering up at the occupants in the room.

'Lunch?' she croaked, her voice sounding as dry and husky as Ethan's had when he had woken up. 'You've got two choices. Roast jungle rat with Kayan root sauce or a selection of meats and vegetable-matter platter.'

Neither sounded appealing to Ethan and he wasn't entirely sure what she was offering. 'I'll have the second one,' he said tentatively, while Mistix had no hesitation in choosing the roast.

The lunch-lady separated two of the black squares and placed them at the front of the tray. The front two tentacles of the creature rose up from below and pointed at the squares, squirting a thick, clear liquid from its tip, covering the square completely. The squares immediately began growing in size, changing shape and colour, transforming into something that was more reminiscent of food.

As this was happening, the next two tentacles of the creature lifted from the floor, leaving it balancing on the remaining pair. Two red rays were emitted, engulfing the developing dishes. There was a scent of cooking in the air as the food started to brown, and a whisper of steam circled in the air, twirling around the old lady like a halo. Ethan was impressed, as in only a few seconds, there sat two plates of steaming hot food, and despite his reservations, they both appeared somewhat tempting. He realised suddenly how extremely hungry he was and sought out which plate was his.

The plate on the left had a mound of brown meat, perfectly roasted and dripping with some kind of dark red sauce. The plate on the right had smaller mounds of food; meat that was white, brown or pink in colour, as well as various vegetable pieces which were green and pale orange. Ethan assumed that his was the one on the right. He would have taken it but had reservations about getting too close to the thing that was carrying his offering. He studied the tentacles, noting the purple suckers on them, which led right up to the body of the creature. It looked completely organic, but after what he had seen, Ethan had to rationalise that it must be some kind of robot. And this was the second type of animal-like robot he'd seen; Budgie being the first. He couldn't help but wonder whether this was the first time he'd ever seen something like this, or had he been completely used to them and just forgotten? A sense of despair swept through him, acutely aware of how lost he was.

He didn't have time to think for too long, as the lunch lady snapped at him to take his lunch. He quickly took it, as did Mistix, and settled the plate on his lap.

'Enjoy your meal,' a monotone voice said, although it didn't come from the old lady, but rather from the creature that had cooked it.

'And hopefully *you'll* have a better outcome than one of the last patients in this room,' the lady said slyly, not particularly sounding as though she meant it.

Ethan took the bait. 'Really? Why… what happened?'

The woman shook her head, as though remembering an unfortunate incident.

'He was about your age. Came in to get a mole removed and contracted a skin infection. It covered half his body in the end, so they had to amputate both arms and a leg.' She gave a sneer as though the thought of it was particularly distasteful. 'He used to sit up in that bed, just watching the infection creep up his arms, eating him alive.'

She turned to leave, her 'food trolley' also scuttling in an almost comical fashion with legs flailing, to re-arrange its position in the opposite direction. 'It's something to think about, I suppose.' She smiled broadly, showing an assortment of crooked and black teeth before leaving the room.

Mistix gave a hoot of laughter. 'Stupid old crow!'

Ethan looked tentatively down at his bed,

horrified that he could be sitting in a cesspit of germs.

'Relax!' Mistix crooned. 'Bacteria can't grow in here; she's making it all up. I'm sure her twin is much… nicer.' He seemed to choose his words carefully and looked pointedly at his brother. The meaning wasn't lost on Kredax, the word 'nicer' also obviously referring to him as though it were an insult of some kind.

Ethan looked down at his food. 'There's no cutlery.'

Kredax looked kindly at him. 'Just say what you want and open your mouth. It'll go in. They use plate technology here.'

Ethan stared at him. 'Plate technology?'

Kredax nodded. 'The plate that the food is on uses exon beams to lift the food and direct it into your mouth. Just don't close your mouth at the last minute or it'll end up all over you.'

With some trepidation, Ethan thought he'd try the vegetable portion first.

'Green vegetable… thing,' he ventured, and quickly opened his mouth. The mound of green food immediately rose off the plate and shot into his mouth. He choked uncontrollably, splattering some of it back out again. Mistix laughed while Ethan tried to compose himself.

'You'll get used to it,' Mistix purred and focused on his own dish.

'Leg portion,' he demanded. A section of the mound of meat tore off and flew into Mistix's open mouth. He chewed on it hungrily, licking some of the sauce off his lips.

Ethan felt frustrated as he wiped the last of the food remnants from his mouth and pushed the tray away from him. He suddenly felt compelled to get out of the room, a sense of claustrophobia sweeping over him.

'What's out there anyway?' he asked, eyeing the door as though it were an escape from his confused situation. He jumped off the bed and took the few steps to the door. It slid open and a wave of fresh cool air embraced him. He gazed up and around him. He wasn't sure what he expected, but what he saw took his breath away.

Directly in front of him was a service desk, singularly manned by an older lady, who looked somewhat stressed as she was deep in conversation with a patient sorting out an issue. But to the right was a short corridor. At the end of this he could see masses of people passing, hurrying in all directions, a hum of voices floating towards him. Above the crowd flew an assortment of birds similar to Budgie, scuttling around the air like incessant bees, zooming in and out and diving down to inspect the people below.

Ethan made the few steps to the end of the corridor, only to be greeted by a bird suddenly swooping down and hovering in front of him. Its markings were different to Budgie's, being mostly green in colour, but it also had the ability to extend its eyes out of its sockets. The bird appeared to scrutinise him, its rotating eyes strangely hypnotic, before the eyes retracted and it zoomed off again, apparently satisfied nothing untoward was happening.

Ethan stepped forward, staring at the huge, glass-domed ceiling in the distance above him. Sunlight was streaming through, warming the top levels of the hospital which gleamed incandescently. He estimated there must have been at least sixty levels, presumably full of patients, or at least patient rooms. The area at ground level in front of him stretched some fifty metres across and twice as wide. The floor was marbled, gleaming white and reflecting the never-ending footsteps stomping across it. Ethan surmised it must be the main foyer area of the hospital. The chaos of the people and security birds had him entranced, and all he could do was watch and stare. And despite the obvious presence of the birds and the close proximity they had to the people, nobody gave them a second glance, even as they hovered within touching distance. Everyone seemed totally at ease with them.

But as he watched through the crowd, he gaped as he saw twins everywhere. Two young boys passed to his left, arguing, while behind followed their identical mother and aunt, also having a disagreement. To his right were two older, large ladies, jostling each other as they tried to fit in between the oncoming people. Everywhere there were twins. Dressed the same or dressed differently; same hairstyles or deliberately not. The faces were duplicated in all directions; a sea of repetition which did not seem possible.

Astounded, his attention was finally drawn towards three figures moving towards him. It was their garb that stood out, as they were dressed totally in long, black, floor length robes with hoods to cover their heads. The edging of the hood was white, but from his distance the faces beneath were concealed.

Yet it wasn't their appearance which caused Ethan to feel uneasy; it was the way they moved. They walked in unison, each step moving in tandem with the next, their bodies moving so smoothly it gave the impression of gliding. They moved with purpose and direction, arms folded at their chests, their heads totally in line with each other.

'I'm sure they're Nuns,' Ethan muttered to himself, intrigued not only by these strange figures, but also as he could recognise what they were. Did this mean he could remember people or objects from the past, even if he could not remember a specific encounter with them? He wasn't sure.

The figures came closer and their faces became clearer. They looked around sixty years of age, the wrinkles on their faces clearly evident, although giving no suggestion of any emotion or thought. Each was expressionless and focused on the route ahead of them. As they were about to pass him, their heads simultaneously turned, piercing eyes bearing down on Ethan. Their soulless stare froze him, and as he watched, just for a second, he thought he saw a red glow emanate from beneath their hoods. Their heads turned away once more, and they disappeared into the crowd. Ethan had the strongest feeling something about them was not right. There was definitely something odd.

Ethan decided to follow, setting off through the people, dodging to the left and right as he tried to follow the direction the Nuns had gone. It didn't take him long to realise, however, that he had left his run too late, as with the masses of people around him it proved to be an impossible task. He was also feeling a bit giddy after his exertion and thought he'd better rethink his actions. He stopped, intrigued by a notice board of some kind on the wall to his left. It was flashing up images every ten seconds or so, but the information was actually embedded into the wall rather than on a separate display. He read the advertisement that was currently showing.

Just because you are characteristically challenged, it doesn't mean you can't contribute to society in a meaningful way. Contact Jackson's Abattoirs today by Tele link.

This ad melted away and another replaced it.

Have you been Time Leech tested? Remember, you won't know they are there until your final moments of life. Have the best death possible. Contact Time Leech Removalists today. Squeech the leech!

A third notice flashed up.

Reports of space chip usage confirmed. Report any vanishings to security immediately.

Ethan felt a presence at his shoulder. He turned to see Kredax standing there, apparently having followed him from the hospital room.

'You should come back to the room,' he suggested. 'The nurse was looking for you.'

Ethan nodded, but asked, 'What's a space chip?'

Kredax glanced at the notice board. 'It was a very old device used to keep criminals on the straight and narrow. It was a chip implanted directly into the brain. If the criminal performed an illegal act, the chip could be activated, and it would immediately transport the person by materialisation to security.

The pain of transportation was often enough to deter them from any more criminal activity. It was banned ages ago; there shouldn't be any left in existence.'

'But they are being used now?'

Kredax nodded. 'Seems like it. Several people have just vanished into thin air.'

'And what about Time Leeches?'

Kredax shrugged. 'Some people think it's just a marketing ploy, but the evidence seems irrefutable. There are invisible beings who attach themselves to a person, feeding off their life force. The host doesn't know they are there except feeling slightly more tired than they should be, but the Leeches' main aim is to be there at the host's death, sucking the last moments of life from them, making the death experience extremely painful. They also tend to get impatient the longer the person lives and can subtly hasten the person's likelihood of dying.'

'How do they do that?'

Kredax looked unsure. 'Influencing the host's thoughts, causing them to make wrong decisions or create confusion, nobody really knows, but enough of the population is worried about it to make their eradication big business. A lot of people are making a lot of money from it.'

Ethan looked from Kredax to the people rushing past him. A woman was hurriedly pulling her two daughters along beside her. The girls' extended free hands each had an image of a dog floating above it. The dogs were bouncing around playfully and barking, apparently to the girls. Another man passed, a translucent newspaper hovering in front of his eyes as he walked, an image apparently projected from a disc on his forehead. Ethan's head began to spin. Why was everything so alien to him? Why didn't he know any of what he had just been told? The whole world around him was so completely foreign. He looked back to Kredax, bewildered and confused. Letting out a gasp, his legs began to buckle as he clutched at Kredax's clothes for support. Kredax tried to hold him but he was already passing out. His eyes lost focus and slowly he slid to the floor.

CHAPTER 3

Ethan was back in his bed. The difference now was that the lighting was dimmed. A figure hovered above him, momentarily causing Ethan alarm before realising it was Sebastian.

'It's okay,' the nurse whispered reassuringly. 'You passed out, but you'll be fine. We still don't know what's wrong with you but we're working on it.'

Ethan was in no mood for platitudes. 'How do you know I'll be fine if you don't know what's wrong with me?'

Sebastian seemed unaware of his terse reply. He removed some kind of circular electronic device which had been placed around Ethan's head.

'We'll do some more tests in a few hours. It does appear you had traces of a potion in your blood stream which could account for your memory loss. Do you remember taking anything?'

Ethan stared at him in the subdued light. 'Obviously not,' he said drily.

Sebastian laughed nervously. 'Of course. Sorry. I'm just about to finish my shift. We've had all sorts of problems today. A patient had an overdose of a weight loss potion; he was air-lifted in by a couple of security birds. Another patient was administered an illegal mind-altering potion; he thought all the security birds were attacking him. And one of the plate technology plates in the hospital developed a fault, throwing food at a patient who ended up being cornered in his room, covered from cranium to toenail in mashed elder-puppy flesh. If it's not one thing or another, it's a gadget that's gone wrong.'

'Gadget?' Another word he did not understand.

Sebastian nodded. 'Yes, you know.' He re-assessed his words. 'Well, maybe you don't. The gadgets are the little devices that people play with, you see them around everywhere. Or they can be used to help people, like clean windows or pick up leaves at the front of your house. Mostly they are there for amusement.'

Ethan didn't know what to say about that. He didn't really care, he had other things on his mind.

Sebastian pulled out a vial from his tunic pocket. 'Now take this potion for tonight. It'll give you a good night's sleep. I'm going off duty until tomorrow.'

Hesitating, Ethan took the potion, unsure if he wanted it, and pulled himself upright. 'Sebastian. Do you know anything about a group of Nuns around here?'

Sebastian appeared to flinch slightly before smiling. 'I believe they share a convent at the back of the hospital. I… haven't had a lot to do with them.'

'What do they do?'

Sebastian made a face, as though not really wanting to talk about them. 'Keep to themselves mostly. I see them pass through the hospital sometimes. They're not really… my type of people.'

'Do you think they are evil?' Ethan tried to read between the lines.

Sebastian held a finger to his lips. 'We are not supposed to discuss that topic. It's illegal. People's genetic predisposition is their own business.'

Ethan wasn't to be put off. 'But you would realise about people, once you get to know them, exactly what… type of person they are.'

Sighing, the nurse agreed. 'Yes, sometimes. But we all try to get along anyway.'

He turned to go.

'May your twin…' he started automatically, before stopping himself. 'See you tomorrow.'

Ethan watched him leave, the door sliding shut behind him.

'Why would an evil person want to get along with a good person?' he asked himself, perplexed.

He looked over to Mistix's bed. The figure lying there appeared asleep, the covers rising and falling in a rhythmically slow motion. Ethan still held the sleeping potion in his left hand. He looked at it for a few seconds before deciding it was not something he wished to have tonight and pocketed it in his trousers.

Taking a deep breath and evaluating that he was no longer dizzy, Ethan left his bed, crossed the room and snuck through the door, trying to be as quiet as possible.

The main foyer was much more subdued now. A few people scuttled past but compared to earlier it was dead. He could only see one security bird in the distance, which seemed to be looking in his direction. Ethan wished to ignore it and turned away, but the bird flew over, hovering in front of him. Ethan instantly recognised the patterns of colour and realised it was Budgie.

'What do you want, Budgie?' Ethan asked, still walking forward.

'I don't want anything,' Budgie replied with an affronted tone in his synthetic voice. 'I was merely going to enquire how patient five was feeling.'

Ethan was surprised. 'Oh. Okay. I'm fine thanks.' He didn't know what to say next, so he asked the bird how he was. Budgie's eyes seemed to widen in delight.

'Nobody has ever asked me that before! I can give you a complete analysis of all my systems, particularly those relating to human-like interaction personality data chips and subfolders. I think you will find those astonishingly interesting.'

Ethan grimaced a little and quickly said 'No, that's fine, Budgie. I'll just accept that you are… okay.'

Budgie seemed to frown, the area above his eyes distorting slightly. 'It's no trouble. I'm happy to do it.' There was a subtle tone of annoyance in his reply. Ethan wasn't sure how to proceed without insulting the bird further but decided that a question of distraction may work.

'Have you caught any criminals lately?'

Budgie's head tilted to one side.

'Please define lately. Do you mean in the last twenty-four hours or within twenty-four to one hundred and sixty-eight hours? If it's more than one hundred and sixty-eight hours I would recommend using another term other than lately.'

Ethan stared at him, not particularly interested in defining his question.

'I don't know. The last twenty-four hours.'

'No criminals have been apprehended.'

Ethan managed a fake smile. 'Okay. Great!

Everyone's behaving then.'

'I would not agree. Although no serious offence has been observed, I have noted inappropriate conversations taking place.'

There was a pause, and Ethan wondered whether he was referring to Sebastian's remarks earlier. Whether he did or not, Ethan didn't care to continue the conversation with the automaton. His interest in the bird suddenly fell to zero as he saw, towards the far corner of the foyer, a robed figure moving with purpose towards a corridor down the left-hand side. Ethan didn't know why the Nuns intrigued him so much, but he felt compelled to know more about them.

'Well, I should go,' he announced to Budgie, already setting off. 'Have a good night.'

'May your twin be with you always,' Budgie happily replied.

Ethan grimaced. 'Yeah. You too.' He wished he wasn't constantly reminded that he should have a twin somewhere. To think that there could be somebody out there, like him, who knew everything about him; it was hard to digest. It gave him hope, but at the same time he didn't want to think about it. Not until that person was standing in front of him.

As he walked away, he could hear the bird saying that strictly speaking he had no twin, although the other automatons could in some respects be considered as twin-like due to the similarity between them. Ethan had to smile despite himself. Budgie was definitely annoying but also strangely endearing.

He quickened his pace across the marbled floor.

On his left he saw the notice board he had looked at earlier and his eyes automatically read the inscription flashing up.

Need a private investigator? Jessica can find what you are looking for.

There was more writing, but Ethan had hurried past, intent on finding out where the Nun was going. He argued with himself as to why he was following her in the first place. Was it just because the Nuns looked odd? Was he just curious? Bored? Maybe all three. Perhaps Nuns had always intrigued him, but then again, he couldn't really remember if that was true or not. His useless memory was frustrating him. Could that be what was driving his curiosity? The more he saw of the world around him, the more chance he had of something triggering a recollection from his past. At the moment he was struggling, desperate for anything he may recognise which would make him feel like he had a link to reality, instead of the nothingness which followed and lived inside of him now.

Ethan reached the beginning of the corridor the Nun had ventured down and saw the back of her robe sweeping away from him some small way ahead. He quickened his steps, eager to get closer, but quietly, as he didn't want to be seen. He noticed a number of doorways as he hurried by. Some were opaque and looked different to the door of his own room, so he assumed they may be offices or something else rather than a patient's room.

The corridor was long, very long, and even though the ground was flat, Ethan had the feeling he was going downwards. He wasn't, of course, but the sensation was tangible, and the light seemed to lose its gloss, no longer the brightness of the hospital foyer, but a darker, slightly eerie light which had lost its sharpness. He became aware of his own breathing, which made him realise that he was feeling slightly anxious, even though he had no reason to be.

Ahead of him the Nun had reached the end of the corridor, breaching its confines and entering a larger open space. She continued onwards, apparently oblivious to the company she kept, which somehow gave Ethan a sense of satisfaction. He was a few moments behind her, reaching the corridor end and pausing to take in the new environment.

Tall trees stood in front of him, astonishingly high considering they were still inside the hospital, although he wondered whether he had actually left the building to reach an outside area. He couldn't tell as he could see no ceiling or sky. The trees were dense, with some areas covered in a lower canopy of branches and leaves which gave a more claustrophobic feel. A pathway lay in front of him, winding its way through the trees which seemed to draw the light from the air, tempting him with what it concealed. Ethan smiled wryly to himself, knowing full well he was going to take the bait and also aware as to how different it would look in daylight, which would make a mockery of the trepidation he felt now.

Looking left and right he stepped out onto the pathway, noting that there was no obvious sign of life around him. He assumed the Nun had followed the path, so he stepped forward, lightly moving once more in her tracks. The path itself was made of small pebbles and they rustled slightly as he walked. He stopped to check whether he could hear the Nun up ahead but there was only silence.

Moving once more, he continued on while glancing to either side, past bushes and trees which he imagined could conceal any number of beings or beasts. It occurred to him that due to his lack of memory, he wouldn't have any idea of what could live in a forest anyway.

He ventured further away from the relative familiarity of the hospital, until eventually, through the trees, he saw the shape of a building, looming up out of the semi-darkness. The dark grey stonework of the front façade reached upwards, contrasting the width which was quite narrow, giving the impression that it was towering above anybody who stood before it. A large wooden door, slightly ajar, was set at the front, above which sat two stained glass windows. The windows were in the form and pale grey colour of the faces of two Nuns, staring outwards as though keeping watch over anyone who may approach the convent.

Ethan walked slowly up to the building, repeatedly glancing up at the Nuns' faces, whose black eyes seemed to warn him that his presence may not be welcome. He approached the door, listening intently for any sounds and tried to peer through the crack as he got closer. There did appear to be a faint light inside, but certainly he could not see or hear anything from where he was. Reaching out, he placed his right hand on the door in preparation to give it a slight push so that the gap would widen, when suddenly he heard something. He jumped in alarm and turned around to see the Nun standing immediately behind him.

She stood facing him, her hands clasped in front of her. Up close he could see every detail of her hooded face; the blackened eyes which stared, the pale, wrinkled skin which barely concealed the congealed veins underneath, the formless lips which were no more than a slit in her head. Ethan was shocked by her appearance and automatically opened his mouth to say something but was stopped in his tracks as her lips moved and formed a smile. But it wasn't a smile that was pleasing. It appeared forced, her features seemingly unaccustomed to forming such a shape and gave no comfort to Ethan that she may be friendly. But before she spoke, Ethan was momentarily distracted by her teeth. They were gleaming white and absolutely perfect. The contrast between her teeth and her face was almost comical as the two could not have been more different. She would have had the most brilliant smile if only she knew how to do it convincingly. Presently her teeth were gritted together, the corners of her mouth pointing upwards as she tried to give the appearance of pleasantness.

'Hello, young man,' her gravelly voice whispered, a glint in her eye unnerving him. 'Can I help you?'

Ethan could feel his tongue getting tied even before he spoke.

'Oh, I er… was just… seeing what was out here.' He didn't know how convincing he sounded; he wasn't sure he would have believed himself!

'We don't get a lot of visitors here,' the Nun continued, sounding like she was perplexed as to why people would not like to visit. 'It's such a lovely setting, here in all the big trees.' She glanced upwards, admiring the canopy, the corners of her mouthing stretching a little more as though pleased with what she was seeing. 'But we always welcome visitors who may want to converse, someone to talk to, especially if you may not be feeling so… good about yourself, for whatever reason.' Her teeth gleamed at Ethan, making him feel slightly nervous.

'Are you a patient here at the hospital or just a visitor, seeing some poor, sick friend or relative?'

'I'm a patient here actually,' Ethan replied, before cursing the truth of his statement as it made him feel vulnerable. 'But I'm almost better,' he added, straightening himself up, before his heart jumped as another Nun had suddenly appeared on his left-hand side.

'This is Sister Domenicas,' the Nun explained. 'And I am sister Charity.'

Ethan nodded slightly. 'Nice to meet you,' he muttered unconvincingly, and then realised there was yet another Nun on his right-hand side, whose approach he had once again not heard.

'So… what do you all do here?' he asked nervously, looking from one to the other, trying to work out if any of them were twins or they all just looked so pale and haggard it was hard to differentiate between them. It was a voice behind him that answered, from yet another Nun who must have come through from the convent.

'We are here for the people,' she said, her eyes wide open and gazing at the boy. 'We are here for the sick and the weak, for the poor and the destitute. Our doors are wide open for anyone who needs a place of refuge.'

The sister on his right continued. 'Our sisters reach across the land, touching the souls of many who seek our contact, placing the needs of the people above our own, paving the way for those lost in lightness.'

Domenicas added almost feverishly, 'We are Sisters, joined in concept with the Sisters of the Living who harbour themselves in other institutions, in other hospitals.'

Ethan was becoming increasingly uneasy, apparently surrounded by a group of ranting nutters.

'So, what do you call yourselves?' he asked pleasantly, while looking for a route of escape without actually setting off in a run.

Sister Charity stepped forward, her face almost touching Ethan's.

'We are the Sisters of the Dead,' she rasped unblinkingly. 'Come inside and we can tend to you. Let us bless you.'

'Yes, come inside,' two more Nuns said together, also apparently having appeared through the convent door.

The Nuns were eager, nodding their heads in unison, trying to encourage Ethan to accept their offer. He was now totally surrounded, six pairs of eyes fixated on him, longing for obeyance.

Ethan didn't quite know what being a Sister of the Dead meant but he felt a distinct lack of confidence that it was something he should find out. The Sisters moved closer, Domenicas reaching out to him, her cold hand grasping his shoulder tightly.

'Come with us,' she whispered, putting pressure on him as she tried to push him towards the convent. The others also reached out, holding his arms, smiling at him, six sets of teeth bearing down on him with the same twisted expression of Sister Charity.

Ethan felt panicked, trying to dig his feet into the ground underneath him, but found he only slid as the pebbles held little grip.

'No!' he commanded, but it had no effect on the Nuns. They pulled harder and whispered in unison with fervent voices, 'Come with us. Come with us. Let us bless you.'

The door to the convent swung open and Ethan could see over the Nuns' shoulders candlelight in the darkness. He tried to resist, but together they were much stronger, somehow holding him fast despite their apparent age. They almost had him across the threshold when a voice penetrated his fear, calling out with feminine authority.

'Stop where you are!'

The Nuns did indeed stop, and everyone turned. A figure was making its way down the pathway, hidden by shadows but then stepping out into the light.

It was a young lady, no more than eighteen years old, holding an extended arm out towards the group as though it were some kind of weapon. She strode confidently towards them, her long, fiery red hair falling past her shoulders and swaying across the middle of her back as she moved, and tall black boots reaching up to below her knee. Her expression was accentuated by heavy make-up, but was resolute and bold, obviously not afraid of the Nuns who had transfixed their cold gaze on her.

'Let him go!' she demanded, then added, 'And go back inside!'

There was stony silence as nobody moved for several seconds, before one by one the Nuns released Ethan, turned, and without saying a word moved back into the convent. The last Nun disappeared, and the door closed firmly with a thud.

Ethan looked amazedly at his rescuer, astounded by the apparent power she had over the Nuns.

'Thank you,' he muttered, holding his shoulder where he could still feel the cold grip of the Nun's hand. The newcomer lowered her arm slightly, and then beckoned.

'Come with me.' Her voice was high pitched and squeaky, almost like a child.

This was the second time today a complete stranger had asked him to come with them, but he was a lot more inclined to go with this girl than with the Nuns.

'Who are you?' he asked, as they moved back towards the hospital.

'I'm Violet,' she said, smiling slightly, before saying incredulously, 'What were you doing down here?'

Ethan felt defensive. 'I was just seeing who they

were. What are *they* doing down here? What do they want?'

Violet frowned. 'Why shouldn't they be down here? Where should they be?'

It was Ethan's turn to frown. 'Locked away maybe; in an institution or prison?'

Violet was taken aback. 'Why?'

'Why?' Ethan asked angrily. 'Didn't you see what they were doing to me?'

Violet shrugged. 'What did you expect? Just because they're not… wholesome doesn't mean they should be locked away. They deserve to have a life. You shouldn't have been wandering around by yourself.'

'Well, I didn't see any signs warning me! Just something simple like 'psychotics ahead, approach with caution' would've done!'

Violet laughed. 'Perhaps you have a point,' she conceded, 'although most people would be a bit more wary.' She glanced at Ethan, a look of intrigue flashing across her face. 'So why weren't you wary? There wasn't even a security bird near you.'

Ethan looked at her blankly. 'I didn't know I had to be.' Violet looked confused, so he explained further. 'I'm a patient here. I've lost my memory.' He looked sullenly downwards. 'Completely,' he added. 'I don't remember anything.'

Violet looked impressed. 'Wow. That's tough, explains a lot.'

Ethan looked up, not sure how to take her last comment, but he still wanted to know more about the Nuns.

'But it's a hospital. Why are they here?'

'As I said, they need to be somewhere. Here's as good as anywhere. You just have to be… careful.'

Ethan nodded slowly, starting to get a sense of the world he was living in. Good and evil living side by side, accepting each other's differences, or tolerating them at least, so that society survives. But how long could such an arrangement last for before… what? Before one gets tired of the other's presence, before co-existence becomes impossible? The bond between twins must be strong, but surely… surely not that strong.

His thoughts were interrupted as they'd now reached the corridor in the hospital he'd walked down earlier, and another girl was walking towards them. She strode purposefully forward, bouncing red hair flowing behind her and over her shoulders, make-up highlighting her attractive features.

It took Ethan a couple seconds to realise who she was. It was surely Violet's twin, but this version was about ten kilograms heavier. Violet was lithe and athletic, wearing a relaxed white t-shirt and casual jeans, while her sister wore a similar outfit although slightly tighter, with flat boots finishing off the ensemble. Both girls, of course, had a collar wrapped around their necks, which was completely at odds with their outfit, and both had a shoulder bag draped across their chest. The newcomer moved in a similar manner to her sister, yet somehow did not exude the same self-confidence.

'Bringing back strays are you, sis?' she asked, not unpleasantly, in the same high-pitched voice as her sister.

'I'm Ethan,' he introduced, managing a smile.

'Rose,' she replied succinctly, also smiling.

'Ethan was getting to know the Sisters of the Dead,' Violet explained.

Rose appeared interested. 'Oh! How did that go?'

'Well, they were encouraging him to go inside the convent when I turned up and asked them nicely to let him go.'

Rose seemed perturbed. 'Lucky.'

'Why did they let me go?' Ethan did not understand. 'Why did they do what you said?'

Violet smiled wryly. 'Well, I have one or two tricks up my sleeve that can be quite persuasive.' She spoke as though she had secrets yet to be revealed.

Rose added, 'And our father and uncle own the hospital.'

Ethan looked impressed. 'So, they are the Sisters' landlord?'

'Not exactly, but they've got a lot of influence.' She smiled. 'We're just going to visit them here in the hospital? Do you want to come?'

Ethan felt momentarily uneasy and looked closely at the two girls. Both seemed friendly and he had to be honest, not unattractive. But with everything he knew about the world around him, one of these girls was bad by nature, perhaps even evil, and here he was, even though he'd only just met them, intending to make friends with them. Was he being naive in even thinking that that was a sensible thing to do? He didn't know the answer to that but given the fact that he was totally alone, any company was welcome.

'Sure!' he replied, finding himself eager to see more of the hospital and also intrigued to meet the hospital owners.

The three of them walked back towards the main foyer, turning off to the right before reaching it. At the end of this corridor was a large set of frosted glass doors, with an embedded insignia emblazoned on the front. It had two arms reaching up at an angle, fingertips touching at the top to form the peak of a triangle. Within the arms sat two hearts, one on top of the other but as mirror images, so that one was upside down.

Violet held her palms out towards the doors and they lifted up and separated, retracting into the wall-space. A blue light formed a curtain in front of them which Violet and Rose walked through. Hesitating slightly, Ethan followed, quite unsure as to what the light was, but apparently it caused no harm.

Emerging on the other side, they had entered an enormous laboratory. On his left were tables and shelving absolutely packed with vials and glassware containing an assortment of multi coloured liquids, powders and solids. On the table closest to them was a small fire, burning out of the table itself but causing no scorch. Above them hung plants from the ceiling, some with long tendrils reaching down while others comprised solely of leaves growing in a clump, without dirt, the roots exposed to the world.

On their right there was also a similar state of disarray, but the shelves and tables were crammed with electronic gadgets, some small, others large, some glowing with an inner light, others emitting various sounds which presumably had a function or use. They were piled on top of each other, sticking out in all directions while others lay on the ground beneath. The whole place looked like a technological and biological dumping ground.

The girls paused, and Rose called out, 'Father!' while at the same time Violet called out 'Uncle Syntax!' The three of them stood listening for any response, and eventually they got it. A loud whistle filled the room and a bright burning light rose into the air ahead of them, behind a particularly high shelf laden with plants. The light could have been mistaken for a firecracker as it hovered in the air with sparks shooting off it, but Ethan was amazed to see that it actually looked like an arrow pointing downwards. The girls moved towards it, dodging around various items strewn across the floor which could either be described as weapon-like or completely unrecognisable as to what function it may perform. The only thing he did recognise was a human leg leaning up against a shelf, electronic wires poking up from the top of the thigh and looking remarkably life-like. As they scrambled past, Ethan had to look twice as he thought he saw the toes move.

Following the girls around the shelf with the plants, they came across a slightly hunched man with extremely long, grey hair, which was curled around and around his head to cover the baldness underneath. He looked to be in his seventies, had a miniscule pair of glasses attached to a band that went around his head and he had the obligatory collar around his neck. He was stooped over a collection of beakers housing blue and green liquids, two of which he held in each hand. Like Mistix, Ethan noticed he had numerous rings on his fingers.

As the trio approached him, he looked at them and uttered the word 'Up!' Ethan noticed the lenses retract upwards out of the way, revealing excitable green eyes. 'I've perfected it!' he said breathlessly. 'Another success!'

Violet didn't seem to hear him, instead focusing on the mass of hair on his head.

'What has it done today?' she said exasperatedly, shaking her head.

'Oh, I know!' he cried, one arm reaching up to touch it. 'It's just got a mind of its own; I really need to fix it.' As if to prove his point that it did indeed have a mind of its own, his hair suddenly started uncurling of its own accord, rising up into the air until it was fully extended vertically, and then just as quickly became limp and fell onto the floor, detaching itself from its owner. His bald head was bald for no more than a second as new hair started to sprout immediately, growing until it covered his head and reaching several centimetres in length. It then grew a quiff at the front, creating an overall effect that was considerably better than what he'd had seconds before.

'I know I've got a potion to reverse it here somewhere,' he spluttered. 'It's getting really quite annoying. It's very hard to concentrate when there's hair shedding in all directions around you.' He brushed some strands off his shoulders. 'I should never have tried that restorative potion in the first place, but never mind, you live and learn.'

He then noticed Ethan for the first time, squinting at him.

'Who's this?'

'This is Ethan,' Violet said happily. 'He's a patient here. This is our father, Camdex.'

Ethan said hello and received a nod in return.

'So, what have you developed now, Father?' Rose asked. Ethan couldn't help but notice a slight tinge of boredom in her tone. Camdex looked distracted as he stared at Ethan, before turning to the girls, excited once more.

'Watch this!' He took hold of a beaker with a murky black liquid inside, un-stoppered it and poured a couple drops onto the table. Immediately, blue smoke appeared, curling itself upwards and a hole abruptly appeared in the table. They could now see right through to the floor. Rose peered at it closely.

'Is it an acid or something?'

Camdex excitedly shook his head, grinning from ear to ear.

'Definitely not, it's better than that. Keep watching!' They all stared at the hole, waiting for something to happen, but as the moments passed, their sense of expectation began to diminish.

Violet pointed out the obvious. 'Nothing has changed.' Slightly frustrated, Camdex took a stirring rod from the table and poked it into the hole. As he moved it around something did happen; a dark swirling mass appeared above the hole, a gaseous cloud which turned faster and faster. The gas was thickening, spinning like a whirlpool until it got sucked downwards and the missing part of the table reappeared, completely surrounding the stirring rod and holding it fast.

'See!' Camdex exploded. 'It just takes a bit of time for the molecules to re-assemble, but the hole is only temporary! It's revolutionary, think of the uses!'

Rose studied the rod sticking out of the table. 'It's pretty cool but what would you use it for?'

Camdex spluttered: 'Well… imagine you wanted a hole… but then didn't… its use is self-explanatory.'

Rose hugged him. 'It's amazing, you're a genius. Don't tell Uncle Syntax or he'll find some way to neutralise it.'

'Bah!' Camdex spat. 'This potion would be too advanced for him. After fifty years he's still floundering around trying to keep up with me with his technological gadgets. Potions from the earth will always supersede wires and man-made components.'

Rose sighed as though she'd heard it a hundred times before.

'Then why do you make technological gadgets as well?'

Camdex shrugged. 'I'm multi-skilled. And sometimes you need to fight tech with tech.'

A voice behind them made them turn.

'I thought it was the other way around. You're the one who's floundering around trying to oppose what I develop. You've always been scared of what I may achieve!'

Syntax stood several metres away, seemingly at the boundary between his collection of inventions and Camdex's collection of plants and potions. Syntax was slightly hunched like his brother, dressed in a black laboratory apron and carrying an expression of distaste. He was mostly bald with tufts of dyed black hair at the back of his head and above his ears, while on the top of his head sat a strange looking, opaque glass hat, attached tightly to the skin beneath. It was the first thing Ethan noticed about him, and as he stared at it, he thought he could just make out the shape of something inside.

'Me, scared?' Camdex exclaimed. 'Of your inventions? Like a house mouse is scared of a block of cheese. And by that, I mean a block of cheese that has no scary attributes whatsoever!'

'Cheese doesn't have any scary attributes, Father,' Rose said wearily.

Camdex looked surprised. 'Really? Well let me show you my home-made, protein digesting cheese; if you touch it, its digesting enzymes will start eating your finger. You need to eat it with a fork and be really quick to swallow. I'm sure I've got some around here somewhere.' He turned towards his assortment of biological treasures behind.

'We don't need to see it,' Violet cut in. 'We know what cheese looks like. We grew up with it, remember, you kept feeding it to us.'

Camdex smiled appreciatively. 'Well, I've always looked after you girls as best I could.'

'Yes, we know,' Rose said kindly, her face grateful.

'And because you keep reminding them,' Syntax sniped, before looking Ethan up and down, a strange look on his face. 'Who's this boy?'

Violet introduced him again and explained what had happened at the convent. Syntax smiled slightly, nodding in understanding as though he would have expected nothing else.

'Not the smartest of things to do, was it?' he judged harshly, although speaking in a somewhat flippant tone. 'The Sisters of the Dead are a fascinating group, totally intriguing to watch and completely independent of the outside world. Ever since they…' Syntax seemed to search for the correct word. '…arrived,' he continued, 'I've observed them, but without going inside their convent it's hard to see everything they do. It's a pity you didn't go inside.' His face lit up at the thought, although with a touch of sadism. 'It may not have been… beneficial for you, however.' Ethan could almost see Syntax imagining what might have happened inside the convent, and he found himself getting uneasy. It hadn't taken Ethan long to make up his mind as to who was good and who was evil out of Syntax and Camdex, and consciously decided that he wanted to stay in Syntax's company for as short a time as possible.

'Well, I've learnt my lesson,' Ethan said succinctly, his face impassive.

Syntax's eyes twinkled. 'I'm glad to hear that,' he said smoothly. 'In a world such as ours, you really do have to be careful where you go and who you talk to. You just never know when things can go wrong.' He spoke as though his words had hidden meaning, a tone that was not lost on his brother.

'Cut the crap,' Camdex blurted out, just as his hair grew several inches at the front and tickled the end of his nose. 'You're too old to be melodramatic trying to scare people, especially when I'm around to stop you. And don't think that extra bit of brain on top of your head is going to help. You may as well be growing cheese for all the good it will do. I know you too well. I can make any potion to counteract your technological trinkets or protect against the Nuns.' As if to prove a point he pulled several vials off one of his shelves and pushed them into Ethan's hands. 'Here! If they bother you again throw this at them. One will freeze them and the other…' He paused and frowned, concentration taking over his slightly withered features. 'Well, I don't really remember what this one does, but if you use it just make sure you step back a bit.'

Ethan looked at the girls as if questioning whether he should hold onto the vials or throw them away immediately. Neither seemed eager to give him encouragement either way, with both turning to Syntax to see his reaction. The other brother said nothing, remaining silent for several seconds before reaching into his pocket and pulling out a small device. He held it in the palm of his hand as though he'd never seen it before. It was a sphere that appeared scaly and glistening as though wet, with its green surface reflecting the light. Eventually, Syntax spoke.

'I too have developed something new, something completely fantastic which would leave *your* potions for dead.' He paused, perhaps to allow his brother some time to develop jealousy over this mysterious invention. 'Six months of work and it's a success.

Technology reborn. Only a mastermind could have developed it. My never-ending patience through the years is reaping its rewards.' Syntax appeared clearly satisfied and was obviously gloating.

'I've heard that before,' Camdex said sceptically.

'What does it do?' Rose asked.

Syntax turned the device in his hands, rolling it as though it were a magical orb.

'It's the only one of its kind and has the capacity for great… change.' He chose his words carefully. 'Much more useful than making holes.' He looked deliberately at the table Camdex had used his potion on previously. 'But it's not something I wish to share… yet.' He turned to the two girls who were looking both intrigued and inquisitive.

'I may tell *you* later.'

Ethan couldn't see who he was looking at, whether he was talking to both girls or to just the one. Perhaps he had a stronger connection with one of them, because one was evil like himself. But the girls were different to Syntax and Camdex, or indeed Mistix and Kredax. As far as he could tell in the short time he'd known them, there was nothing to differentiate the two between good or bad. They both seemed so… normal. They were a couple of girls who were friendly and apparently caring, and certainly Violet may have saved his life. Did that mean she was the good one? But then Rose didn't seem bad and he found it hard to imagine that she was. He began to question what Kredax and Mistix had told him; perhaps not every set of twins *were* good and evil. He was a bit perturbed, however, having met two of the girls' relatives. Their father was dotty if not mad, and their uncle was likely mad in an evil sense, who he could imagine laughing maniacally as he told everyone that 'nothing could stop him now!' while he attempted to destroy the world.

Ethan suddenly felt compelled to find an excuse to leave.

'I should get going,' he announced somewhat conspicuously, clearing his throat in an official manner. 'The nurses must be wondering where I am.'

'We can take you back,' Rose offered, apparently eager for his company.

Ethan noticed Syntax smile. 'Yes,' he said quietly. 'You had better get back...' Still smiling, he turned and left, disappearing back into his jungle of inventions, his voice calling out to the girls that he would see them later.

'I'd better get back to it as well,' Camdex informed them, a frown on his face. 'I need to work out what your uncle has developed and make a potion against it!'

He turned and picked up a small package, pushing it into Violet's hands. 'Here's some cheese, you never know when you may need it.' He then pushed the hair out of his eyes and waved at the group, before turning to leave as well. As he left, they could hear him muttering 'The outside looked like it was made of illuminous metal. Very rare indeed... yes, very rare...'

The two girls and Ethan headed back the way they came, passing the 'leg' with the protruding wires once more. Ethan paused in front of it, studying it closely this time.

'It looks real,' he marvelled, reaching out to feel it.

'Don't touch it!' Rose squealed, pulling him back so that he almost lost his balance. He looked at her for an explanation.

'It's not fully… disconnected yet,' she justified.

'So?' Ethan asked. 'What does that mean?'

Rose continued walking. 'It means it still has some sensory input. Best leave it alone.' She made no effort to clarify this, and Ethan was left perplexed as to the meaning of her answer. His curiosity was not satiated however as he noticed three stationary figures draped in floor length cloths close by.

'Your father makes statues?'

Irony clouded Violet's features.

'Not statues exactly; more like relatives.' She tugged on one of the cloths and it slid off, causing Ethan to stare in disbelief. It looked like a real person; in fact, he was sure it was a real person, but the man appeared to be totally frozen, staring ahead in a lifeless gaze.

'Meet Uncle Phoenix,' Violet introduced. 'He's not as chatty as he used to be but if you press his nose he'll talk.' To demonstrate she pushed them tip of his nose and the lips began to move.

'I don't feel well.'

Ethan grimaced. 'It's a robot?'

Violet shook her head. 'No. It *is* actually Uncle Phoenix. Uncle Syntax used to have a taxidermy business. Before people passed away, he would take recordings of them saying various sentences and then integrate the recordings into their preserved bodies after they died.' She pressed the nose again.

The pale lips moved again. 'Is that a cat on the wall?'

'Uncle Phoenix was one of the first and was a bit confused when they took his recordings as he was close to death. Usually though it would be a recording that would remind the relatives of their loved one. You know, something that would be characteristic for that person to say, so for the relatives it was almost as though they were still alive.'

'There was quite a demand for it at one stage,' Rose added. 'But then people became fickle and it went out of fashion.'

'It's… amazing,' Ethan said with trepidation, quite certain he would not want one in his house. If he had a house, that was.

Rose explained further.

'Our father and uncle have been in their laboratory for fifty years. This is just one of hundreds of inventions. It's been their life.'

'They don't seem to get along,' Ethan noted.

'Well, most of what they invent is to counteract the other's inventions. It's a perpetual contest to see who is the smartest between them. Of course, they are probably just as smart as each other, being twins, though neither would admit it.'

'But don't be fooled,' Violet added. 'They may fight but they need each other, it's always been that way. They are evenly matched.'

Ethan couldn't help himself. 'Like yourselves?'

The two girls looked at him, the same expression on their faces.

'Are you both even?' he clarified. 'The same?'
'Of course,' they both said calmly.
'We are twins,' Rose said matter-of-factly.
'And you both get along?'
'Very well.' Violet smiled. 'There's no reason why we shouldn't, none at all!'
'But…' Ethan began, but then he didn't know how to phrase his next question, although Violet had anticipated what he was asking.
'Not matter who we are biologically, there's always free choice. We can be who we choose to be, decide what to say and what to do no matter what other… instincts may suggest.'
The two girls spoke together. 'Life is a choice.' He had the impression that their simultaneous sentence was a result of not only because they knew each other as twins, but because they had spoken that phrase many times before.
Ethan nodded, accepting what they had said, and found that he couldn't help but be intrigued by these girls. And he knew he wanted to know more, although perhaps he hadn't even realised why. He did, however, still have one burning question to ask the girls.
'Your father said your uncle is… growing a brain under that thing on his head?'
Rose grimaced. 'Yeh…,' she drawled. 'I think he wants to get ahead over our father. It's a bit extreme…'
'Just a bit?' Ethan said sarcastically.
'It's genius!' Violet interrupted. 'Though it wouldn't be to my taste.'
'It looks a bit ridiculous,' Rose added, apparently

understating the obvious. 'If you look really closely though,' she leaned forward as if telling him a secret, 'you can see what he's thinking.' Ethan's eyes met hers, the graveness in her gaze making him unsure as to whether she was serious. That was, until a faint glimmer of a smile broke her steadfast features and she turned away. Ethan couldn't help himself but to also smile, the first smile he'd had since opening his eyes in this world he did not recognise.

'Is there a hole in his head?' he ventured light heartedly.

'Not really,' Violet answered. 'The new brain is growing on top of his head, there's only a small connection to his original brain through the cranium. The neuronal cells are multiplying underneath the protective capsule in a completely sterile environment, as its bathing in antimicrobial plasma.'

Ethan had to admit he was impressed but revolted at the same time.

'And this is just to be smarter than your father?'

'Basically,' the two girls said at once.

'And is he?' Ethan queried.

'Smarter?' Rose said. 'I haven't noticed any difference.'

'Me neither,' Violet agreed.

Ethan contemplated the situation with a certain curiosity. If the aim was to become smarter than his brother, then he would probably not want to reveal his increased intelligence deliberately. Not until he had a reason to, perhaps by inventing something far superior to his brother. Could that have been what he was showing them, and if he is indeed the evil twin then could it be something dangerous? Ethan suddenly began to feel worried.

CHAPTER 4

The trio had made their way back across the hospital foyer, Ethan directing them towards his room. The crowds of people had returned, and the golden rays of sun were warming the upper levels. The birds had also reappeared, following the masses of people wherever they went. One figure in particular caught his attention; a lone Nun, crossing the foyer in the opposite direction to himself, likely heading back to her evil coven at the back of the hospital. They stared at each other, before she became disinterested and broke their mutual gaze. Ethan subconsciously made a face of disgust, imagining her cold hands on his shoulders.

Re-entering Ethan's room, the trio saw Mistix sitting up in bed being tended to by Sebastian. Kredax was hovering in the background.

'I think you're fine,' Sebastian was saying. 'I can't see anything is wrong with you.'

The nurse turned as they entered, and a look of relief flooded his face.

'I'm glad you're back, I thought I'd have to go out and get you.' He motioned towards the bed. 'You should rest; I'll just check you over.'

Ethan lay down on the bed while Sebastian placed a square disc on his forehead. It glowed an iridescent blue, while he noted readouts on a device in his hand.

Violet and Rose had introduced themselves to Mistix and Kredax. Ethan couldn't help but notice how they all appeared to be summing each other up, carefully noting what they could about each other. Ethan surmised it was probably a ritual here that everyone performed, as they made silent judgments on who was likely good or evil. He noticed in particular the curious look on Mistix's face, whose eyes darted from one girl to the other, and who quite possibly was taking more interest in them than he should have done. The reason for this was lost on Ethan, or perhaps he was letting his imagination get away from him as he didn't trust Mistix no matter what he did.

Sebastian straightened up and peeled the disc off Ethan, his manner more officious than he had been previously.

'Everything looks stable, you seem to be recovering.' Ethan noted Sebastian's change in his tone, as though he knew something.

'You've got some test results back?' Ethan, too, took on a serious manner with his question.

Sebastian confirmed it with a nod.

'Yes.' He glanced around at the spectrum of people in the room. 'Would you like some privacy while I tell you?'

Ethan looked around at the faces peering at him. The two girls he'd barely known for a couple of hours, their faces beaming at him which somehow warmed him inside; the two guys who were so opposite to each other that the difference almost scared him, who also he barely knew and, in the case of Mistix, he wasn't sure he wanted to. And then Sebastian, the person who had cared for him as was part of his duty. A collection of people he hadn't known twenty-four hours ago. Or, at least, he didn't as far as he remembered. Did he mind if they heard important, private information about his health? He had to admit that no, he didn't mind, because if it was something really bad, then they were better than no one.

'No, it's fine,' he stated sullenly. 'You can tell me.'

Sebastian nodded again and drew a breath, positioning himself closer to the boy.

'As I said, you don't appear to have any permanent damage so any dizziness you still feel should settle down.' He hesitated, apparently trying to form his words.

'So, what caused it?' Ethan prompted, willing Sebastian to talk faster and explain himself.

Sebastian pursed his lips and said quietly but clearly, 'You've got something inside your brain that shouldn't be there.'

Ethan stared at him while Sebastian continued.

'It's been placed between the frontal and parietal lobes causing some displacement but appears to have integrated itself into your neural network. We're not sure but... we think it's a space chip.'

He stopped to let this sink in. Ethan said slowly, 'A space chip?'

Sebastian nodded. Ethan looked to Kredax, fear joining the abundant mixture of emotions he was experiencing.

'But that's what *you* told me about!' he exploded. 'It was on that news flash in the foyer. Why is it inside *me*?'

He wanted an answer desperately, but Sebastian just shook his head.

'We don't know. Nobody knows what their purpose is or where they are coming from or who's behind it. You're the third documented case apparently. There will be some officials from the Society coming to see you in the next few hours.'

Ethan was struggling to believe what he was hearing, and felt his face become flushed with anxiety.

'How did it get inside me?' he demanded, frantic for answers. 'Did they cut me open?' He ran his hands through his hair, searching for any evidence of wounds or scarring.

'No,' Sebastian reassured. 'The device is materialised directly into the brain. There doesn't need to be any surgery. At least, that's how they used to do it to criminals.'

'I'm *not* a criminal!' Ethan shouted.

Sebastian touched his shoulder to try and calm him. 'We know. It hasn't been used for that purpose for many years. However you got it, it was completely unauthorised.'

Ethan began to panic.

'What's going to happen to me? What will it do?'

He heard in the background the stale voice of Mistix reply.

'You will probably disappear. That's what happened to the others.' He showed no sign of sympathy with his comment. Kredax glared at him disapprovingly.

'We don't know that,' he said quietly, trying to soften the blow.

'Then why put it in? Sooner or later, it'll be activated and off he'll go, transported to wherever they want him to go.'

'Who's they?' Ethan snapped.

Mistix shrugged. 'Well, that is the interesting question. Who wants you, Ethan, and why? What have you done to deserve that much attention?' He sneered slightly. 'Oh, I forgot. You don't remember.'

Ethan's dislike of Mistix was growing stronger and he would have retorted a reply if Rose had not spoken up.

'Perhaps it's random. There could be many other people affected who don't know about it yet.' Her high-pitched voice seemed higher than before, as though agitated.

'No, this was deliberate,' Ethan rationalised, turning to Sebastian. 'You said there was also a potion in my bloodstream, somebody drugged me. Somebody is after me.'

Sebastian indicated agreement.

'When the Society arrive, they will try to help you. They may have methods to remove it.'

Rose spoke. 'Or study him like a laboratory meer-rat,' she said softly in her squeaky voice. All eyes turned to her as she explained. 'If the chip activates, they might be able to trace its source which could be more use to them than removing it. Can we count on them to help you?'

Ethan considered what Rose had said and somehow it made sense. If he had something in his head the Society wanted to know about, could he trust them to help him? He had no idea, but he had thoughts of the Nuns and wondered if he would get a similar treatment by this group.

Kredax spoke. 'The Society would be your best chance of getting it removed, they have nearly every potion and device in existence at their disposal.'

'Providing they want to use it…' Violet added.

'There's no reason why they wouldn't,' Kredax defended.

'I'm just not sure,' Rose replied. 'It's up to Ethan as to what he wants to do.'

Sebastian interceded. 'When they arrive, you can talk to them, I'm sure they will help.'

Their conversation was suddenly cut short as a horrible scream shattered the quiet. This was quickly followed by more shouts and screams, coming from the direction of the foyer. Once again Ethan leapt from his bed, his troubles almost forgotten as the intensity of screams increased.

'What's going on?' Violet asked.

Everyone moved at once, running for the door, pouring out to see what was happening.

In front of them was pandemonium, people running in every direction, falling into and over each other as they ran from… what? It wasn't immediately obvious, until Ethan saw a figure scuttling no more than ten metres away from them. He blinked before realising it was the same creature that had served him lunch; or at least one that looked like it. As people ran past, it reared up on its hind legs and pounced on a nearby man, its six tentacles wrapping around him in a constrictive bear hug. The man cried out in terror as one of the tentacles lifted up and came down on his head. Ethan could see a thick, mucus-like substance oozing down his face, before another tentacle rose up and a fierce red glow enveloped the man. His screams gurgled as he writhed in agony, his arms flailing helplessly in the immovable arms of his attacker. The cries quickly died, however, and he hung loosely in the grip of the creature. The tentacles released their hold and he fell to the floor. Despite the noise around them, Ethan just made out the automated words coming from the monstrosity.

'Enjoy your meal.'

Ethan was aghast, literally unable to move or react, fixated on the crumpled man. A surge of adrenaline shot through him as the creature turned towards them. Rose was the closest and it appeared to target her. It pounced, but what happened next Ethan couldn't take in, unsure if he really saw what he saw. Rose jumped out of the way, but not only did she get out of the creature's path, she jumped completely over it, clearing the top of it by several metres. She landed solidly behind it, unfazed by the huge leap she had just performed.

Not to be outdone, the creature then lunged at Violet, wrapping itself around her tightly. Ethan reacted instantly and ran to help her but hesitated when he saw how calm she was. She raised her arm upwards and pointed directly into the body of the creature. There was a bright flash and the over-developed kitchen hand suddenly exploded, splitting down the middle with sparks shooting off and chunks of tentacle falling to the ground. Violet pushed the body away from her as it slid in its own oozing slime, exposed wires and mechanics clearly revealing its robotic origins.

The next second, they heard the harsh sounds of buzzing above their heads. Rays of heat burst down onto the people below. Ethan looked up and saw a bird, its rotating eyes blazing as it shot forth beams of death. As they watched, the hovering robot tilted slightly and was now facing Rose, the teenager apparently a target once more. Sensing it was about to fire, she leapt to one side, again travelling an extraordinary distance in a single, agile movement. Violet raised her arm and this time Ethan could see clearly a fierce red beam shooting forth from her palm, striking the bird squarely in the chest and causing it to shatter above them, raining down pieces of metal and electronics. Another bird fired, exploding the ground at Violet's feet. She swung around, and her arm flashed once more, obliterating the bird that dared attack her. Ethan stood with his mouth open, staring at her arm which was obviously much more than an arm. His mind raced back to the electronic leg leaning against the shelving in the laboratory and he looked down at Rose's legs, suddenly making a connection. She saw him looking, but above the din of people's screams their attention was diverted by Mistix.

'We should go!' he shouted, moving towards the exit of the building. Another beam of heat hit the wall above their heads, effectively herding them towards the exit anyway. Making an obvious decision, the group, consisting of Ethan and both pairs of twins, began to run. Ethan looked back to see Sebastian leaning over to assist a fallen man and hesitated, but felt his arm being pulled as Mistix tugged him forward. Ethan tried to resist but the other's grip was strong and they were swept away with the crowd.

The light outside was bright and the confusion was tangible. Ethan still had Mistix attached to one arm and he felt Rose's presence beside him. Violet was behind them with Kredax.

'Do the birds usually do that?' Ethan spluttered, completely at a loss as to what happened.

'Not at all,' Kredax replied, obviously just as surprised by the events as Ethan was.

Mistix seemed to know where he was going, leading them off to the right and down a side street. Already the number of people was less here, and as they turned left, right then left again the street became narrower and the crowd was largely left behind. They finally turned one more corner which led to a much smaller alley way which sat almost in darkness due to the shadow of the surrounding buildings. Mistix still urged them forward, stopping at a run-down door with peeling paint.

'What's this?' Kredax asked, suspicious.

'Somewhere to hide,' Mistix explained. 'At least until security manages to get things under control.'

'The security birds were the ones shooting at us!' Violet ejaculated.

'Not all,' Rose informed. 'I saw one bird shoot another. They may not all have had their programmes tampered with.'

'How do you know they've been tampered with?' Ethan asked.

'They must have been, otherwise they wouldn't be shooting people. I can't understand how it could happen. It should be impossible.'

'Something has seriously gone wrong,' Kredax warned. 'It could be a disaster for our whole society!'

'Don't be too melodramatic, brother,' Mistix reprimanded, annoyed. 'It's probably just a few rogue birds which will be quickly sorted out. Your precious society will still be here tomorrow.'

'Speaking of the birds, here comes one now,' Rose warned. They all looked, as one was flying towards them. Ethan squinted.

'It looks like Budgie.'

Mistix placed his hand on the door and it slid upwards into the wall.

'They all look the same so let's not wait to find out.' He moved inside, and everyone followed, Ethan glancing back for a second take. The closer the bird got the more it looked like Budgie, but the door slid shut firmly before he was really certain.

CHAPTER 5

The group were now in near darkness, and the chatter of rowdy voices filled their ears. A few steps further they found themselves in a large bar. People sat around tables laughing and drinking, some obviously under the influence of a concoction from the bar while others sat in more serious conversation. On the far side was a section sealed off with a panel of glass, completely separate to the rest of the room. Ethan studied the clientele. An unshaven man sat closest, with a tattooed serpent on his arm and a ring lodged through his nose. Coupled with the black gleam of his clothes his appearance reeked of malevolence. He chatted with another man with long, greasy black hair and a jacket emblazoned with a creature with four taloned arms and three horns on its head. As Ethan glanced from one person to another, they all emanated the same feeling of hostility and vice.

'It's my local bar,' Mistix explained.

'It's a Snake-shift bar,' Rose said flatly, taking in her surroundings. She looked at Mistix. 'We won't be staying long.'

He shrugged. 'Well, unless you want to fight the birds outside you should probably wait an hour or two at least.' He gestured around him. 'Relax, suck up the vibe, have a drink, chill out, take the weight off your legs.' He glanced deliberately down at her legs. 'Or whoever's legs they are.'

Roses' face clenched tighter. 'They are mine,' she said quietly but just loud enough to be heard above the chatter in the background. 'I had an accident and my father improved them.' She swung her red hair back defiantly, daring him to say something. Instead, Mistix turned to Violet. 'Did your arm have an accident too?'

Violet slowly nodded. 'Actually, yes. It's a bit of an upgrade from the original. Comes in handy sometimes.' She flexed the fingers pointedly. Mistix nodded. 'Sorry to hear you have had so many accidents in your family. At least you're okay now.'

Ethan couldn't tell if he was being genuine or not, as mostly he just sounded sarcastic.

Mistix turned and held up a hand in the air. 'Five brews,' he muttered, even though he was some distance from the bar. It was then Ethan noticed who he was talking to; or rather, what. It was a white humanoid robot behind the bar. He counted six eyes circling its round face and eight flailing metallic arms which were working busily to prepare the patrons drinks. It must have registered Mistix's order as one arm extended over the heads of the people below and reached towards them. Its open palm hovered in front of Mistix's face, causing him to react in a way that so was completely out of character, it caught Ethan off-guard. He smiled. The robot's hand flashed, and an electronic female voice stated, 'Payment accepted.' It then retracted back to the bar to begin preparing the ordered drinks. The group settled down to a nearby table, grateful for a seat.

Ethan looked around at his fellow companions. Kredax appeared worried, unseen thoughts obviously flashing through his mind. The girls were studying their new environment, perhaps, Ethan guessed, more as a strategic reconnaissance to determine potential danger or escape routes than any real interest in where they were. Mistix, on the other hand, appeared relaxed, almost as though he'd enjoyed the excitement they had just endured and was about to enjoy a drink in his favourite bar.

Ethan didn't know what he felt. Everything had happened so fast and knowing that people had been hurt or even killed, it made the sense of loss inside him due to his lack of memory even more pronounced, desperately so. But he knew he just had to keep going, take one step at a time until events sorted themselves out, as he had to believe they would.

Violet spoke across the table to Mistix who sat opposite. 'You come here a lot, then. Why?'

Mistix shrugged. 'It's fun, entertaining, interesting people, what's not to like?'

'Because it's a Snake-shift bar.' This statement obviously spoke for itself.

'What's wrong with a Snake-shift bar?' Ethan asked.

'Apart from the entertainment and clientele, absolutely nothing,' Violet said lightly. 'It's for a certain type of person.'

'I've never been in one,' Kredax ventured.

'No surprises there, brother,' Mistix leered. 'You're lucky they let *you* in.' He laughed.

'There would normally be no reason why I'd *want* to come in,' he responded.

'How do you know if you've never been in one?' Mistix teased.

'It doesn't matter, we're here now,' Kredax

sighed. 'What are we going to do about the birds?'

'Us?' Mistix questioned. 'What's it got to do with us? Let the security forces deal with it. It's not our problem.'

'It was our problem when we're being shot at or trying to be squashed to death and cooked!' Violet interceded. 'They seemed to be targeting us.'

'Yeah, I thought the same,' Rose added. 'Like they were deliberately going for us.'

'Why would they do that?' Mistix said. 'It could have been any of us. It was just random attacks.'

'Maybe.' Violet sounded doubtful. 'But if they try it again, I'll blast them to pieces!'

'That was impressive,' Ethan complimented, 'the way you fought them. No wonder the Nuns left me alone.' A sudden thought struck him. 'How did they know you could do that with your arm?'

Violet shrugged. 'I don't know. They probably don't.' Ethan looked at her curiously.

The drinks arrived, five metallic arms diving in from above their heads and placing the drinks on the table. Ethan looked down at the tiny beverage in front of him, a murky brown liquid in a glass standing no more than three or four centimetres high. A huge handle ostentatiously hung off the side, three times as large as the glass itself. He watched as Mistix thirstily brought the beverage to his lips and took the smallest of sips. His cheeks expanded, and he gave a deep swallow as though he had consumed an entire cup full. Intrigued, Ethan clutched the handle of his drink and took a sip. As soon as the liquid flowed into his mouth there was an explosion of fluid as the volume in his mouth multiplied. He nearly choked, but fortunately the flavour was quite agreeable and he successfully swallowed without any embarrassing spluttering. His taste buds tingled with a sensation of sweetness and richness, and he had to admit that it was actually really nice. A pleasant feeling of relaxation washed over him, and he sunk back in his chair with relief as some of his tension dissipated.

The others reacted similarly to the beverage and the group felt awash with a new vibe, calming their heightened senses after the attack. Ethan turned to Rose who was seated beside him, to see she was already looking back.

'Are you okay?' she asked, in her high-pitched girly voice.

Ethan nodded slowly, acknowledging yes even though it was probably not the most accurate of descriptions.

'Are you? That bird nearly got you.'

Rose smiled. 'It was a bit slow; it had no chance.'

Ethan was impressed. 'Your legs are mechanical.'

Rose nodded.

'And the leg at your father's laboratory, that was the same?'

Rose squirmed. 'Well, actually, that was from my old pair. Father gave me an updated version recently. He hasn't fully disconnected the sensors on the one you saw though so if you'd touched it, I would have… felt it.'

Ethan remembered her panic when he'd reached out to them. 'Oh! Sorry.'

'But this pair is better. They're stronger.'

'It must be sort of… cool to have them. I mean, to be able to move like that.'

Rose half agreed. 'Yeah, but I really have to watch what I eat as I put on weight so easily. Everyone else uses up energy when they walk around, but I don't as my electronics are doing all the work. I need to exercise my arms and core if I'm to keep fit. That's why I'm bigger than my sister,' she added candidly.

'Oh, okay… right.' It was something Ethan would not have even thought of. 'How did it happen? I mean, how did you… lose your legs?'

Rose looked downwards. 'It was an accident. That's all. Accidents happen.'

Ethan raised his eyebrows. 'That's a serious accident!'

'Very unfortunate…' Rose agreed solemnly.

Ethan didn't know if she was being brave with her understatement of the issue or just didn't want to talk about it, but he got the feeling he wasn't going to obtain any more information about it from her.

'Well… sorry it happened.' He smiled consolingly, and she returned it briefly.

He then became aware of a figure hovering beside him at the head of their table. A beautiful blonde lady stood there, her golden hair flowing over her shoulders, her blue eyes smiling at them. She wore a free-flowing cream dress down to her ankles, and a basket hung around her neck full of small statues. A halo of flowers circled her head.

'Hello, everyone,' she said sweetly. 'Sorry to interrupt you all but I have some wonderful statues which I can allow you to purchase.' She smiled engagingly. 'Each one is impregnated with a fortune potion which will bestow the owner with its magical quality. It could be a potion of luck to help you get through hard times, or a potion of health to relieve your ailments, or a potion of affluence for when you are down on your funds. All you have to do is keep it close to you and wait for its influence to bring you whatever you desire. Each one is imbued by hand and can be purchased for only fifteen Trons each, or you can buy three for thirty-nine Trons.' She looked expectantly at the group. 'How many would you like?'

'We don't want any,' Mistix said flatly.

'We have our own potions,' Violet added.

The lady was not to be discouraged. 'But these impregnated statues are not to be found anywhere else, they are truly individual. You won't believe the beneficial effect they will have on your lives.' She draped an arm softly over Ethan's shoulder. 'What about you, young man, perhaps a potion imbued with the power of attraction could be just what you need?'

Ethan looked down at the statues. One was of a hunched over creature holding a heart in its hands. Another similarly repulsive aberration held what seemed to be a human leg bone in one arm. He couldn't imagine what this would signify but it made his decision simple.

'No thanks, maybe next time.' He smiled up at her, hoping she would not be too annoyed. Her response was not what he expected.

She reached into her basket and pulled out a knife, turning the jewel encrusted weapon slowly in her hands, balancing it with not so hidden meaning.

'I can guarantee your purchase will ensure fortune on your lives and will stave off any nasty accidents. It really is a once in a lifetime opportunity.' She held the tip of the knife to her index finger, and a drop of blood oozed from the blade. 'And let's put it this way.' Her tone had changed from sweetness to venom. 'I never leave a table without making a sale.'

Ethan glanced nervously at his companions, wondering whether they had thirty-nine Trons between them. Rose and Violet looked at each other calmly.

'B22?' Violet asked.

Rose shrugged in agreement.

Violet reached into her shoulder bag and pulled out a vial. She un-stoppered it and flicked the liquid contents onto the lady in a single motion.

The potion reached its target, splattering the red colour unceremoniously across her face and hair. Ethan saw extreme anger well up in the beauty's eyes, but she had no time to carry out her veiled threat with the knife. Her mouth opened in a silent scream and her face seemed to cave in, wrinkles spreading ferociously across her features. Her hands became gnarled, clutching the knife as her crooked fingers closed around it. Her blonde hair bleached grey, shortening in length as the tips split and frayed. Her anger turned to shock, her mouth hanging open. Violet got up and pulled the knife from her grasp, depositing it in her own bag.

'Old ladies shouldn't play with knives,' she reprimanded harshly. She turned the old lady around and gave her a gentle push forward. 'It will wear off in a day or two, so think twice about your next sale.'

The lady shuffled off, croaky sobs emanating from her constricted throat. Bouts of laughter followed her, as the man at the table next to them who had seen the confrontation enjoyed the display of Violet's actions. He turned back to his drink, suitably entertained.

Ethan was flabbergasted; it seemed with each passing moment he was more and more surprised by these self-reliant girls. Even Mistix looked impressed.

'Quite a force to be reckoned with, aren't you?' he observed wryly. 'I'd better be careful.'

'Is there a reason why you'd need to be careful?' Violet asked.

Kredax took another viewpoint. 'Will she definitely be okay by tomorrow and back to normal? No side effects?'

Rose answered. 'Yes, she'll be fine. We'd never really hurt anyone.'

Mistix was intrigued. 'Really? Surely one of you would have no qualms in causing a bit of pain?'

Both sisters turned to him, the look on their faces betraying… what? Anger? Hurt? Ethan had trouble reading them but whatever it was, they portrayed solidarity.

'We are not like other people,' Violet said. 'Whatever we do, whatever we say, it's through free choice, not because of any natural instincts.'

'We make decisions based on what is best for both of us,' Rose continued. 'Nothing else matters.'

Mistix was surprised. 'I've never heard anyone say something like that before.'

'Perhaps we could learn from it,' Kredax said pointedly.

'It doesn't mean I believe it,' Mistix retorted. 'To go against your own nature? It would be like tearing yourself in half.'

'Life is a choice,' the girls said together.

'Crap,' Mistix spat.

'You can't be all bad,' Ethan interjected. The table became silent at his blatant admission of Mistix's persuasion. Ethan retreated back into his seat.

'Well, there aren't any birds nearby to hear,' he said meekly.

Mistix drew himself up.

'Whatever I am, I am exactly who I'm supposed to be, not pretending to be something else.' He glared at the girls.

'No matter what the cost?' Kredax asked. 'Or the damage you do to yourself?'

'How can there be a cost, Kredax, with you sitting on my shoulder constantly watching me?' Mistix said smugly. He looked towards the other side of the room and changed the topic completely. 'The show is about to start. This should be interesting.'

Violet and Rose got up simultaneously.

'Time to go,' they both said.

'Ethan, are you coming?' Rose asked. Ethan put down his drink.

'Okay… um, sure.'

Kredax also got up, and so reluctantly Mistix followed.

Ethan stopped at a water tank set into the wall towards the exit. They must have passed it unseen as they'd walked into the bar, and he stared into the murky liquid.

'What's in here?' he asked. A shadow passed across the glass as a figure swum momentarily into view. Everyone peered into the depths.

'It's an intuition fish,' Mistix explained. 'If it looks at someone, it is supposed to be able to tell whether they are good or bad. If they are good, it opens its mouth in a big grin.' Mistix laughed. 'If they're bad, it shows its teeth.' He glanced at the girls. 'Don't look too closely,' he muttered.

The group stared for a minute or two longer, but the figure didn't reappear. As they turned away, two black eyes pressed up against the glass, glaring outwards. The eyes darted to the left, following the group as they moved away. Beneath the eyes the water swirled, a mouth appearing out of the blackness, thin, fish-like lips connecting with the glass. Suddenly the mouth opened. Two sets of sharpened, gnashing teeth pushed forward, voraciously and savagely reaching out towards the retreating group.

CHAPTER 6

A tall, thickset and muscled man came out of the shadows in front of the group on their way to the exit.

'Where are *you* going?' he said gruffly, arms folded and intent on barring their way.

'We're leaving,' Violet said.

Another man appeared, also apparently aiming to stop their departure.

'The show is starting,' he growled. 'You can't leave.'

'Why not?' Ethan asked.

The first man took a step forward and towered over Ethan, maximising his height to be as intimidating as possible.

'Because,' he said slowly, 'that would be rude.' He grimaced with obvious satisfaction at his display of authority.

Mistix looked at the girls.

'What do you say about that?' he enticed, perhaps wondering if they were going to delve into their bags and produce another potion.

Kredax stepped forward.

'It's not worth it. We'll watch the show. It's fine.' He put a restraining hand each on Rose and Violet. 'Let's go sit down.'

Violet raised an eyebrow but then conceded, deciding he was right; it wasn't worth the effort to make a fuss.

They moved back inside and resumed their seats. A voice boomed out announcing the start of the

Snake-shift challenge. It came from a holographic face of a bald, middle-aged man, hovering in the air above the crowd. It flitted across the room and spun around in all directions, vying for the attention of the people below.

'Grab your drinks and take a seat, we're searching for the next Snake-shift winner!' it announced with gusto.

The hologram stopped in front of a customer. A thin blue light scanned the client from left to right. Apparently dissatisfied, the light shut off and the face darted across to another man, and then repeated the same procedure.

'We want someone who's brave… someone with charisma… someone with tenacity…' The face reached the table next to Ethan's and scanned the two men sitting there.

Ethan started to feel nervous. The light was getting closer to him. And he also noticed that despite the face being the most obvious source for the crowd's attention, many clients were not looking at it. Instead, they were looking at him.

'Someone with a good head on their shoulders…' The face suddenly spun around and zoomed right up to Ethan's, making him pull back in alarm. 'And somebody who's expendable!' The scan on Ethan's face flashed red and the whole bar erupted, hoots and jeers filling the place. Ethan glanced sideways, trying to gauge from his companions a clue as to what was happening. Their solemn faces looked alarmed, even Mistix obviously not keen on the hologram's choice. Ethan felt a hand on each shoulder, as the two men at the door had come up behind him, ready to escort him to the front.

'It's okay,' Ethan spluttered. 'You can choose someone else. I'm not feeling lucky today.'

The men grabbed him under each armpit and hoisted him to his feet, the chair behind falling backwards to the floor.

The men grinned at him. 'You've got no choice, and luck has nothing to do with it.'

Rose and Violet looked at each other with alarm; even Mistix and Kredax exchanged glances. The unspoken word was that this was not good, but there were too many people present to try to stop what was happening. They would have to wait and see how events unfolded.

They half dragged Ethan across to the glassed off area and pushed him through the entrance, the panel sliding shut as he entered. He was now completely enclosed in the transparent cage while the entire bar stared at him, leering with anticipation of… what? He had no idea, but the anxiety that was encompassing him told him that he was in trouble. He looked around the glass room. There were three pedestals, one in each corner, except the corner where he stood. Each pedestal housed a red jewel on top of it. Above him hanging from the ceiling was a wooden paddle. It was about a metre in length and covered in intricate drawings of some kind.

On the far side a darkened panel slid back. Ethan waited with nervous anticipation as he could see movement in the darkness beyond. There were calls from the crowd as the excitement was building.

Gradually, something shuffled forward, and a creature was revealed. Ethan stared at it in disbelief. It was no more than half a metre tall and looked like a furry, white ball on two skinny, stalk-like legs. Two round, green eyes were set amongst the fluffy fur, while long lashes accentuated the effect of looking like a child's stuffed toy. It moved by bouncing, the fur moving in rhythmic waves up and down like ripples on a lake as it jumped forward.

The floating head boomed out once more.

'*We* all know the rules, but in case our visitor does not, the aim of your task is to take all three jewels from their pedestals in the allotted time, while our fluffy friend tries to stop you.' He gave a chuckle, which alerted Ethan to the fact that it may not be as easy as it seemed. 'You can use the paddle, if you want to push her away.'

Tiny fairy lights appeared above him, zooming around and around until they coalesced to form the number five hundred which hung in the air, presumably indicating the time for his task.

Ethan looked out at the crowd, and saw Rose pointing upwards, indicating for him to take the paddle. Tentatively he reached up and pulled it from its hook, feeling the weight in his right hand. It was reasonably heavy but manageable to hold. He thought that if he hit this fragile fluffy creature with it, it would do some serious damage.

A loud siren boomed out, and the coalesced lights decreased to four hundred and ninety-nine.

'Your time has started,' the floating head said with relish.

Ethan considered the creature, which in return was watching him. It was bobbing up and down in the one spot, apparently awaiting Ethan's move.

Gingerly, Ethan took several steps towards the closest jewel, keeping an eye on his companion. As soon as he moved, the creature bounced across the room, lodging itself between Ethan and the jewel. Ethan kept walking, and slowly tried to reach over it to the pedestal. Like a petulant child, it butted his arm with its head, pushing him away with almost comical tenacity. Ethan couldn't help but smile at the ridiculous creature, as it looked insanely cute. He tried to move around it, but it started head butting him in the waist, trying to force him back. Laughing, Ethan jumped to the side, spun around and grabbed the jewel from its lodgings. Smiling, he held it up to show the crowd. The crowd roared, some apparently finding it funnier than it should have been, but Ethan felt pleased.

The creature's own momentum had caused it to fall flat on its face, its legs flailing as it tried to position itself upright. Ethan didn't know if he should help it, but his answer came swiftly.

As he watched in disbelief, the fur changed colour and retracted, becoming short and brown. The legs filled out and grew, no longer spindly but rather tough and muscular. The creature jumped off the floor and turned, revealing a hideous meer-rat-like face with long wiry whiskers, sharpened teeth and large, bulbous, purple eyes. It now had three arms, two either side and one protruding out of its belly. Ethan stood shocked, revolted at the creature in front of him, and astonished at how it could possibly have physically changed liked that in a blink of an eye.

It gave a threatening snarl, no longer a harmless ball of fur. Ethan glanced upwards, suddenly becoming acutely aware of the timer having ticked down to 400. With a sense of panic, he realised he didn't know what would happen if he didn't get the jewels by the time it reached zero, and if the revolting transformation of his adversary was anything to go by, he now had a strong feeling he should not find out.

With heightened urgency, he pocketed the jewel and abruptly turned to make a dash for the next one. He heard the creature scuttling and it easily made the distance to the pedestal ahead of him. As Ethan reached out, the three sets of hands tried to slap his arm away, with just enough strength to cause bruising. Ethan tried again, but this time his opponent lashed out and bit him on the arm. Ethan yelped in pain and in an automatic reflex he took a step back, grasped the paddle and smashed the creature in the shoulder. The momentum knocked it off balance and Ethan took his chance, snatching the second jewel with anxious desperation. A trickle of sweat ran down his cheek as he checked the clock; two hundred and thirty. He only had one more jewel to get.

He heard growling and the creature was changing again. Pocketing the second jewel he turned towards the last pedestal. He failed to notice a leathery tail lash out at his legs, tripping him as he moved forward. He fell face first and the paddle left his grasp. Scrambling across the floor, he reached for his only protection and turned to face the new creature leering over him.

It had now grown to the size of a man, with a smooth, shiny, leathery, black head and an elongated jaw filled with teeth. Its eyes were still purple, but its body was graced with sporadic grey hair. It stood on its two legs with a long black tail whipping back and forth behind it. The growl emanating from it was guttural and menacing, and Ethan had no illusions that a bite from this version could be dangerous if not fatal.

The crowd had become louder, sensing that blood was going to be spilled. Ethan was now covered in sweat, his heart pounding in his ears and his skin tingling with adrenaline. He backed up against the wall, preparing for an attack. The creature lunged, and Ethan forced the paddle forward, catching it in its open mouth and knocking it backwards. It tried again and once more, Ethan diverted its head to once side. Taking a deep breath, he tried to clear his head.

'You know what,' he muttered through gritted teeth. 'I've been doing this all wrong.' He lowered his paddle to one side. 'I'm sure I used to be a cricketer!' He had no idea if this was true or not, but in this time of crisis it gave him inspiration. Holding the paddle with both hands, it was his turn to lunge forward. He struck the creature on the side of the head, as though hitting a ball for six. Several teeth were smashed out of its mouth as it crashed to the floor. Wasting no time, Ethan lunged towards the furthermost corner where the last jewel waited.

He was barely within an arm's reach when he felt a pressure on his left leg. Something had wrapped itself around it. Once more he fell, no more than a metre short from his prize. The growling he had heard before was now replaced with an evil hissing, and the hairs beneath his neck collar tried to rise.

Turning his head, Ethan was now confronted with a huge serpentine abomination, the final manifestation of the Snake-shift creature. Its long, scaly body curled up behind its raised, sleek head, venom dripping from its collection of fangs. Its underbelly writhed in a mass of elongated tendrils, several of which now entwined Ethan's legs. They were tightening, pulling him closer to the nightmare in front. Ethan tried in vain to release himself by smashing the tendrils with his paddle.

His companions in the audience had now stood to attention, acutely alarmed at the dire predicament Ethan was in. The rest of the crowd was enjoying every moment; the bloodlust was tangible.

'I've never seen a Snake-shift that big!' Mistix exclaimed.

'Do something!' Kredax cried out. 'We have to do something!'

The girls agreed. Enough was enough. Violet extended her arm and a sizzling ray pierced the air, shattering the glass barrier in an explosion of shards, covering those closest. The Snake-shift turned, aware now that its confines had been destroyed. The bar erupted as people scrambled in panic for their nearest exit. Rose crouched down and jumped, easily clearing the people and tables next to them, and landed halfway across the room, closer to the Snake-shift. She had a potion in her hand and threw it at the serpent, creating an explosion which burst over its skin. Violet continued her volley of attack, trying to avoid those running across her path.

Mistix and Kredax had also moved, forcing their way through the crowd towards Ethan. The Snake-shift was maddened, though held back by the onslaught from the girls. Ethan still struggled with the tendrils, hitting them repeatedly but with difficulty from his position on the floor. His terror was also being heightened by the noise and explosions around him. Suddenly he felt the paddle being pulled from his hands as Mistix stood above him. Instinctively Ethan recoiled, unsure as to what was going to happen next, but with a strong and swift movement, Mistix brought the tip of the paddle down in a cutting motion, slicing the tendrils in half. Ethan was released and with relief Kredax heaved him to his feet from behind. The Snake-shift was obviously in pain, hissing as it lunged once more at Ethan. With remarkable reflexes Mistix diverted the attack, striking the creature on the tip of its pointed face. The Snake-shift recoiled, its massive tail whipping violently, knocking over tables and chairs. Specks of blood flew through the air. Although its skin was tough and resistant to Violet's attack, it was not impenetrable, and blood was oozing from its damaged torso.

Rose threw another potion, setting off a huge billow of smoke which gave cover for the boys to escape from the area. There was now nobody left at the bar, everyone having fled.

'Over here!' Rose yelled, indicating what appeared to be an exit on the far side of the bar. The group made for it, scrambling over the destroyed furniture, vaguely aware of the floating head shouting out protestations at the destruction of his business. They raced down a short corridor before reaching a door. Mistix placed his hand on it but nothing happened; it remained steadfastly shut.

'It's not working!' he exclaimed, trying again. They heard a noise and

turned back to see the Snake-shift slithering down the corridor towards them, tendrils flailing on either side. Its purple eyes were constricted, focused on its targets, venom dripping as though paving the way for its torso. With only a few metres to go, it opened its mouth to strike.

Violet crouched down. She knew she only had time for one shot. Raising her arm, she fired straight into the mouth of the creature. The effect was instant, its head lolling violently backwards and flailing haphazardly, before its great body crashed to the ground, splattering blood at their feet. Its fierce eyes clouded, and slowly double lids glided over them, forever blocking out the light.

As they watched, the form of the Snake-shift started to transform. Its features blurred and changed, diminishing in size and reverting to its original state. In front of them now lay a pathetic and sad sight; a bloodied ball of white fur, small and insignificant compared to the monstrosity it had been only seconds before. The relief was palpable, but Ethan could not help but feel sad for this creature which had been used so mercilessly for the entertainment of the patrons.

Behind them, the door slid open and the light of a new day beckoned.

CHAPTER 7

The spent group could see and hear the last of the bar patrons as they moved away, some still running, some injured, others casually making fun of the likely fate of Ethan and the destruction of the bar.

Ethan couldn't believe how much had happened in such a short time, and he was very aware of the debt he held to the people standing next to him. The mere fact that some kind of fate had brought them all together meant that he had survived; if they had not been at the hospital, he would have been powerless against the attack.

'You saved my life!' he exclaimed, addressing the group. 'All of you, thank you.' He ran his hand over his sore arm where the creature had bitten him, and anger began to replace fear. 'What the hell was that snake thing? Is that meant to be entertainment?'

'That's what happens in a Snake-shift bar,' Kredax said disapprovingly, with more than a hint of disgust in his voice.

'It doesn't usually end like that!' Mistix interjected. 'And the Snake-shift is not normally that large!'

'Who cares!' Violet snapped. 'I should blow up the place.'

'Well, you virtually did,' Mistix said with amusement.

Rose had gone over to Ethan to inspect his arm, noting the puncture marks and blood that was running out of it. She reached inside her bag and pulled out a vial.

'Hold still,' she said softly, and gently poured the brown liquid onto the injured area. It seemed to find its way to seep into the wound itself, running across the skin and solidifying to form a scab on top.

'It won't take long to heal,' she explained. 'Just don't knock it.'

Ethan smiled wearily. 'I'll do my best.'

Meanwhile Violet was holding up her robotic hand, an image projecting into the air, hovering above her palm.

'Father!' she called out. 'Are you there?'

A blurred figure appeared before his features became defined. It was Camdex.

'Yes?' he asked, hair sweeping down one side of his face. 'Did you forget something? Do you want some cheese?'

'No, Father. I just wanted to see that you are both okay?' Violet explained.

Camdex looked confused. 'Yes of course. Why wouldn't we be?'

Violet sighed. Trust her father to not be aware of the trouble just outside his laboratory, and in his own hospital.

'Some of the birds went crazy and started shooting people. Stay inside the laboratory.'

Camdex was taken aback.

'Really? How extraordinary. I didn't hear a thing. Oh well, they can't get in here anyway, not with my defences. I'll call security and find out what's happening.'

'Fine, be careful. May your twin be with you always.'

'Oh, I hope not,' he replied, and the image promptly disappeared.

'He's fine,' Violet stated unnecessarily.

Ethan had now turned from the group and was staring up the alleyway. He was surprised to see an animal of some kind on nearly every building. Gripping the side of a wall on his left, a large lizard was staring at him, its reptilian eyes darting back and forth, noticing all.

To his right further down, a small dog was peering out from behind a bin, stationary, just watching. And again, on the next building, perched on a balcony railing, a cat had its back arched, head turned towards them, apparently frozen, focused on what they were doing.

'There are a lot of animals here,' Ethan commented, intrigued.

'They're not animals,' Kredax explained. 'They are monitors… cameras, set up by the security forces. It's another way to keep an eye on everybody, apart from the birds.'

'We get watched wherever we go?'

'Mostly, but not completely. And it still doesn't stop all crime, especially indoors.'

Ethan nodded, and then his eye caught something of interest.

With the onset of a new day some businesses had opened. A flashing light was floating around the entrance to one of the smaller buildings, spelling out *Jessica – Private investigator.* The building was sandwiched between two tall skyscrapers, a rustic abode in a jungle of concrete. The door was wooden and had several small windows either side. Wood panelling adorned the walls, and two weather beaten steps led up to the entrance.

'I saw the ad for this in the hospital,' Ethan murmured. 'It's a private investigator.'

'So?' Mistix asked.

Ethan grinned. 'It's just what I need.' Setting off, Ethan made a beeline for the investigator's quarters, his companions following not far behind.

Stepping into the office, a musty smell embraced them and tickled Ethan's nose instantly. Like the outside, the room was unassuming, with a single desk and chair placed in the centre, the desktop uncluttered, apparently waiting for business to create some mess. The walls were slightly more interesting as behind the desk there flashed apparent news articles. Ethan noted that like the notice board in the hospital there was no evidence of where the light for these images was coming from. The first headline screamed out in large bold writing *Middle aged detective foils youths* and next to it a second article read *Criminals be afraid: Jessica is watching.*

The adjacent wall was lined with shelves which had an assortment of trophies and awards, the largest one catching Ethan's interest. It was a cloaked figure holding a giant magnifying glass to its eye. He could just make out the inscription underneath: *Detective of the Year 2120.* It seemed Jessica was quite accomplished in her field of work, a fact which drew surprise as he laid eyes on the detective herself.

She had shuffled into the room from a doorway in the far left-hand corner. She was a middle-aged lady with a firmly set purple perm hanging slightly lower than her collar at the back. Her clothes were relaxed, wearing a white blouse and blue ankle-length skirt, though it was her pink fluffy slippers that drew Ethan's eye. They appeared too large for her, which perhaps accounted for her shuffling gait.

Bright button eyes greeted them as she gave a welcoming homely smile. She held in her arms a large silver tray which had piles of cakes, biscuits and other delicious looking sweets which attracted the teenagers' gaze immediately.

'Hi,' Ethan said reservedly, tearing himself away from the sweets. 'I was looking for Jessica.' He smiled apprehensively. 'I need a detective.'

The lady nodded encouragingly. 'Of course you are! Well, that's me. But let's get onto that a little bit later shall we, there are much more important things to address.'

She waved the tray in front of them. 'Cakes! Now these are all home-made, kids,' she started explaining, as she laboriously managed to wrangle the tray onto the desk. 'I always bake my own desserts, especially for potential clients, as I find it gives a more authentic impression. Not like these other detectives who buy half a dozen cowberry cakes from the local Eleven to Ten-fifty marts. If they treat their clients with scrappy food what are their detective skills going to be like? Half standard.' She looked up at the group, and after several seconds of silence Ethan realised she was actually waiting for a reply.

'Oh, yes definitely,' Ethan spluttered, searching for something intelligent to say. 'I would think that… yes.'

Jessica beamed and pointed a finger at him. 'I thought you would, a smart boy like you. I'm sure you could see through the deception of those without morals, or those with something to hide.' She perused the group of teenagers in front of her as she spoke.

'You're lucky you caught me; I was almost about to pop out for a few minutes to get my hair done. It's getting a bit long, I really don't like it when it touches my collar; it's not very professional!'

'It… looks alright,' Ethan said meekly.

Jessica clasped her hands together.

'Well, aren't you a treat, so lovely. Now I want all of you to try my cakes, don't be shy… wolf them down!'

The group did not need any further encouragement as all were starving. Jessica watched eagerly as everyone reached for a portion of something delectable and chomped into it. Ethan took a slice of some kind, red in colour and creamy to taste. He noted both girls took a piece of cake with a greenish tinge to it with white icing while the other two boys took a brown biscuit each. The general consensus was that the desserts were fantastic, and they needed no encouragement to have a second portion.

Ethan was watching Violet, who looked like she was mentally summing up the fluffy-slippered woman in front of her and trying to reconcile the fact that she was an established detective.

'Do you work alone?' Violet ventured, licking icing from her upper lip.

Jessica gave a warm smile. 'Of course, dear! I

don't want other people interfering and taking me down false trails. No, no, no, that would do no good at all! To have a clear mind you need to *know* your own mind and be confident to pursue your own truth. Other people can be so… distracting… and cause you to lose focus… and… oh look, your friend has just bitten into the sweet, honeyed centre, isn't it just marvellous! That's my favourite one of all!' Kredax now had the sweet centre running down his chin and he proceeded to wipe it up with the back of his hand.

'It's really great,' he agreed. 'You're an amazing cook.' He smiled at this grandmotherly figure, who was beaming back at him.

'Well, apart from catching criminals it really is my second favourite pastime!' she exclaimed, apparently overjoyed to be sharing this information.

'I don't want you to catch a criminal though,' Ethan blurted out, suddenly becoming serious. 'I want you to find out who I am!' The desperation in his voice cut through the frivolity, and he became the centre of attention. 'I don't know who I am,' he repeated, looking squarely at Jessica. 'Can you help me?'

Jessica smiled and reached out to his hand, cradling it in hers.

'Why don't you tell me all about it? It sounds like you have a story to tell. I do have one question though.'

'Yes?' Ethan asked.

'Are you able to pay?' She spoke lightly, as though still talking about her cakes. Ethan's face dropped.

'I didn't think about that. I just saw you here, and thought… well… I guess I can't really…'

Kredax spoke up. 'It's okay, I'll pay. You can pay me back when you find out who you are.'

Ethan looked at him gratefully and didn't even consider saying no as he knew he had no choice.

'Thank you, Kredax. I *will* pay you back.'

Violet, who was dubiously staring at Jessica, spoke up.

'Let's not rush into this. Let's go back to the hospital if it's safe and see if they have more information.'

Jessica moved to face her, kindly wrinkles spreading down the side of her face.

'You're not sure about me, are you, sweetie?' Jessica said pleasantly. 'Perhaps you're thinking 'what can a doddery, middle-aged lady like myself do to help'? You know, the thing that I have learnt above all else, is to make sure my eyes and ears are always open, even when eating cake, and other nice treats,' she added.

Her tone became slightly more officious and controlled, and she spoke with a tinge of authority as she slowly paced the room.

'In my opinion, I don't think you have all known each other long, except for the brothers and sisters in the room, that is. You stand apart from each other and have minimal eye contact. When I mentioned your friend had bitten into that lovely gooey centre, you weren't sure who I meant, as you don't consider the people here your friends.' She was looking at Violet. 'There is, however, a very strong connection between you and your sister, evidenced by your close proximity to each other and your simultaneous reaching for an identical piece of cake. The boys, however, stand apart, and this one,' she indicated Mistix, 'reached for the biscuit first. And then this one,' she gestured to Kredax, 'copied him, not because he particularly wanted that biscuit, but because he wanted to share the same experience as his brother; he is trying to get closer to him, possibly with not a lot of luck. The poor boy here,' she looked sadly at Ethan, 'just chose what he wanted, having had little interest in what the rest of you were doing. He feels very alone right now. But above all this, sweetie, the most interesting thing that I noticed…' She whirled around in her fluffy slippers and pointed straight at Violet. Her wavering finger then dropped, moving down Violet's legs, before she finished her sentence. 'Are your shoes!' Her finger wiggled at the apparent offending items, and for some reason there was absolute silence in the room. Something flickered across Violet's face, and Rose's head turned a fraction as though to look at her sister, but she did not. Mistix's eyebrows furrowed and Kredax looked perplexed.

Jessica smiled. 'They are lovely… of course.' Her finger dropped, and she clasped her hands in front of her.

'I really am quite good,' she said immodestly.

Ethan gave a nervous laugh, trying to disseminate the tension that had suddenly swept through the room.

'I'm convinced,' he stated. 'I'd like to hire you.'

Jessica reacted happily, giving him a grandmotherly hug.

'Wonderful! Now tell me everything about your

unfortunate circumstances.'

Ethan nodded, and quickly recounted the events of the last twenty-four hours from the moment he woke up in the hospital. Jessica nodded in total understanding as concern and empathy reflected on her face. When Ethan finished his story, Jessica slowly shook her head in visible sympathy.

'What a terrible situation you are in. You certainly do need some help.'

Ethan couldn't help but smile, not only due to the cheerfulness of this woman, but because standing before him in fluffy slippers was the opportunity he needed, a chance to delve into his past and find out the truth. Encouraged, he looked at his companions, but was greeted by a set of blank faces. Or were they blank? They were just… different. Different to what they had been only moments before, and Ethan wondered whether he had missed something.

CHAPTER 8

Leaving Jessica's agency, Ethan wrapped a communications device she had given him firmly around his wrist. She had called it a wrist-o-gram. It would enable him to keep in contact with her, just as Violet's hand had contacted her father. A small blue light on the side indicated that it was switched on and open for communication. A thought had started to bug Ethan and he knew he needed to get it off his mind. Addressing the group, he pointed out that they probably had better things to do than to help him, so if they wanted to go their separate ways he completely understood. Secretly, he was hoping Mistix would take the hint and perhaps the girls might stay, but surprisingly they were all willing to continue to support him, or at least hang around him a bit longer. Besides, Rose noted, they needed to work out their next step which would probably include returning to the hospital.

Their decision-making process was interrupted by an agitated voice from above. Budgie had flown in and was flapping his wings excitedly.

'Attention! Attention please! You are required at the hospital immediately; the Society has arrived and wishes to speak to you. Patient five, expediency is recommended.'

The group was wary of the bird, but it showed no sign of a threat.

'What's happening at the hospital?' Kredax demanded. 'Why did the birds attack people?'

'And the food trolleys,' Ethan added, not really knowing what their correct name was.

Budgie bobbed up and down in mid-air.

'The situation of aggression has been controlled. There is no data as to the cause.'

'No data?' Violet exploded. 'You don't know why?'

'That information is currently unavailable,' Budgie said defensively. 'Everything is back to normal now. Please return to the hospital.'

'How do we know we can trust you?' Mistix said drily. 'You are a bird after all.'

Budgie's eyes widened in horror at having been subjected to such an insult.

'I am not in the habit of displaying a non-security bird emotion such as falsifications! The very thought would cause termination of my neuronic drive! It is not possible!'

'Is it possible for security birds to start shooting at people?' Mistix pointed out.

Budgie faltered. 'The random units have been terminated. No correspondence will be entered into.' He turned to leave. 'Return to the hospital. May your twins be with you always,' and flew off.

'Do you want to go?' Rose asked Ethan, who stood contemplating his situation. He made a decision.

'They could be able to help me. I have to see what they say.'

'And if they want to hold onto you as a research project?'

Ethan pursed his lips. 'Then I hope you've got

some more potions in those bags of yours.'

Rose looked uncertain. 'Attack the Society? They are powerful.'

'So are you,' Mistix complimented, a statement which somehow un-nerved Ethan.

Rose turned to Mistix. 'Would you help us escape if we had to?'

Mistix raised an eyebrow, as though the thought hadn't occurred to him. He seemed to consider, before smiling. 'Why not, could be fun.'

'To be on the run from the Society?' Kredax said incredulously. 'It's not a good option.'

'It may be the only option,' Ethan said, 'for me anyway.' He paused. 'You don't have to be involved.'

Mistix reached out and slapped his shoulder.

'Well, you can count on me,' he said and beamed at the rest of the group. 'What about everyone else? Is everyone in?' He spoke as though daring them to say no. He was to be disappointed if so.

'It seems we are in this as a group,' Violet said solidly, and Rose assented. The group looked at Kredax, who appeared to be deciding. Eventually, he nodded and agreed. Ethan's spirits felt raised, happy to have support around him and somewhat energised to face whatever the Society had to offer. And yet, somewhere in the back of his mind, he also felt troubled by their support, but could not understand why.

The short journey back to the hospital was made in silence, everybody carefully watching what was happening around them. Birds flew above as normal and people were on the street, although a silent tension enveloped everyone, furtive eyes checking all directions for trouble or unusual activity.

As they entered the hospital foyer there was a distinct lack of a crowd as would be normal, and instead there stood a number of security personnel, evidenced by their crisply cut grey uniforms and hands weighed down by multitudes of rings, presumably some of which were weaponry. There were no birds inside which somehow was comforting and un-nerving at the same time.

To the left was the spot where they had seen the man attacked and fall to the ground and where everyone was subconsciously drawn to stare. It had been roped off with two men either side, each grasping a complicated piece of electronic equipment positioned on tripods. One man nodded at the other and they switched the equipment on, creating an eerie purple light which encompassed the area between the two. Holographic figures appeared, frantic and desperate, running and panicked, people falling over each other. Ethan recognised what they were seeing.

'They're recreating the attack from yesterday,' he said in wonderment, fascinated yet feeling his anxiety growing. As they watched, the scene unfolded just as they remembered, and Ethan's stomach knotted as he saw himself and his companions embroiled in the assault. Violet's arm flashed, and Rose escaped her attacker with extraordinary ability. Ethan noticed the surprise on the men's faces creating the scene as they saw this, and Rose and Violet quietly spoke in unison.

'Let's go before they recognise us and ask questions.'

As they turned to move off, a man and a woman stood in front of them, barring their way although not in a menacing manner.

'Thank you for returning to the hospital,' the man spoke. 'I am Ledren and this is Firella. We are from the Society of Technology and Potions. We are here to help you, if we can.' He smiled encouragingly, as did Firella.

Ledren was a man of around fifty years, tall and wearing an imposing outfit of a white and black checked coat falling halfway to his knees, a broad brimmed hat to match, black trousers and a collar around his neck which was twice the usual width. Despite his soft words his eyes held the weight of authority, and the lines etched across his face revealed significant experience and patience.

Firella also reeked of influence and power, her dominant forehead highlighting her swept back hair. She too had a high collar from her heavy blue coat which draped steadfast to the ground. Standing as tall as Ledren, they looked a formidable duo.

'You must be Ethan,' Firella said, extending a welcoming hand. Ethan nodded and introduced his companions.

'What happened here must have been very distressing for you all,' Firella continued. 'Ethan, we'd like to have a talk with you. I'm sure you have some questions and perhaps we may be able to answer some of them. Will you come with us?'

Ethan hesitated. 'Where to?'

Firella indicated a double entranceway to the side of the foyer.

'We can talk in there, and then if you agree we can go back to the Society's headquarters.'

Ethan seemed unsure. 'Can my friends come?'

Firella assented. 'Of course.'

Without waiting for further discussion, Firella led the way across the foyer, through the doors and into a comfortable rest area. It was a large room covered in plush floor coverings and interspersed with colourful padded couches; luxury seating for those in need of relaxation. Firella motioned for everybody to sit down, and Ledren closed the double doors behind them. The group waited expectantly for one of them to speak. Ledren took on the task.

'In recent times, our city, our society has been holding onto stability and peace, despite the conflicting nature of the inhabitants. It has not been easy to obtain this balance, a balance which has been brought about through our technology and power. The use of the birds, the integration into society of all types of people regardless of who they are, the constant surveillance and monitoring, the security forces, the system is robust. It has never been subjected to… interference in the past.' Ledren looked grave, his eyes shouldering the weight of his words.

'And yet, there has been interference. The corruption of some of the birds and hospital equipment here yesterday, was in addition to other smaller incidences that have been occurring over the past few weeks. Not only with the birds, but other terrible acts of deliberate…' He paused, trying to find the right words. '…manifestations.' He spat the syllables out with repulsion, before continuing. 'We were able to recover this image from the retina of a man who was killed.'

He held up his hand. Ethan noted that each finger bore a heavily set ring of some description. A yellow ray shot out from one ring on his middle finger, producing an image in the air. The sight was horrifying, as now in front of them was a large, black, worm-like creature. It loomed towards them with a huge wide-open mouth housing several rows of sharp, razor like teeth. It looked like it was about to swallow them.

'Time Leeches!' Ledren spat. 'They have been pulled from their ethereal realm and given full corporeal existence in our world. Their bodies have appeared as flesh and blood in order to attack people in the street. In the past they have only ever been psychically linked to their victims, never becoming a physical being. Somebody has developed a way to pull them into our world to kill.'

This information weighed heavily not only on Ethan but the teenagers as a whole. Seeing these creatures for real meant that there was yet another danger for the population as they lived their everyday lives.

Ledren had been pacing up and down during his speech. He now took centre stage next to Firella, who continued the dissemination of knowledge.

'And now we also have the activation of space chips. A chip, which, as you know, Ethan, lies within you.' She looked down sympathetically at him, and he felt his stomach churn at the thought.

'These have not been used for a very long time

and their implantation is a mystery. How did it happen? When and for what purpose? We don't know, but we do have evidence of their activation, at least for one person.'

She now held up her hand which was also laden with rings and from one there projected a holographic scene of a woman in a park. A boy stood next to her. Although no sound could be heard, the woman suddenly opened her mouth to scream and a blue glow encompassed her and the boy, a light emanating from her head which reached some several metres in circumference around her. The woman was obviously in severe pain as she clutched her head in agony and fell to her knees. There was then a bright flash and the woman and boy vanished, completely disappearing. The group sat shocked, contemplating that this fate was in store for Ethan.

Firella continued. 'We believe the birds, the Leeches and the space chips are linked. Someone or some people have developed a way to manipulate them, to do what should not be possible.'

'Not only that,' Ledren said gravely, 'but we also believe the incidences so far were only tests, randomly propagated in preparation for the real event.' He paused, as though almost afraid to say his next words.

'An onslaught onto our society the likes of which we have never seen. If all the birds became hostile and all the Time Leeches were released into our world, the devastation would be unfathomable.'

There was silence from his audience as the ramifications sunk in.

'Can you turn off the birds?' Ethan eventually

suggested hopefully.

Ledren shook his head. 'Without the birds the… immorality of our world would rise up and cause chaos. Robbery, violence, murder… they occur, but are mostly kept in check.' He gave a long sigh. 'But the main problem is… we don't control the birds.' He paused. 'We don't know who does.'

Mistix gave a sneer. 'Most people think that the Society control the birds.'

'I'm aware of that,' Ledren said abruptly. 'Although we didn't start that rumour, there seemed no point in denying it.'

'How long ago did the birds arrive?' Ethan asked intrigued.

It was Rose who answered.

'About forty-five years ago. At first there was just a few of them, but within a year they were everywhere.'

'And the immunisation program that changed everyone's genetics?' Ethan asked.

'That was close to seventy years ago. Everyone is taught it in school,' Rose explained.

'So, the birds were created to keep everyone from fighting, once the twins had grown up,' Ethan reasoned.

'Yes,' Ledren agreed.

'And the space chip?' Ethan asked. 'How does that fit in to everything? Can you… get it out of me?' He looked earnestly at Firella and Ledren. There was an uncomfortable pause.

'Once the space chip materialises into the brain, it integrates itself into the surrounding brain tissue, into the cells,' Firella explained. 'Essentially it grows.' She took a deep breath. 'We would be able to map the exact dimensions of the chip and dematerialise it out of your brain.'

Ethan felt a sudden surge of hope, but Firella's comforting words did not match her ashen composure.

'The… confounding factor is that once the chip is removed, the cells it had integrated with would no longer be intact. You… would not survive.'

Ethan's stomach dropped, and his hope rapidly disappeared like one of Jessica's cakes.

Ledren spoke. 'Come with us back to the Society. We can do our best for you.'

Ethan hesitated, his fear of being kept as an experimental subject resurfacing. 'Do what?' he asked. 'If you can't remove the chip…?'

'We can do some more tests and have a better understanding of its structure. There may be some potions which can assist.'

Ethan felt flustered, unsure of his next move. Should he trust the Society or listen to the concerns of his companions?

'I… um…' He started to answer, but then stopped in sudden surprise as he saw movement at the back of the room. There was another door through which somebody had just entered, and his heart skipped several beats as he saw who it was.

It was a Nun, one of the Sisters of the Dead. And she was followed by another one, and then another, until there was a continuous line of Nuns entering the lounge, gliding towards them, wearing the same expressionless faces he had seen before. The door he had entered through also opened and more Nuns piled in, all staring straight at the group. Ethan felt a coldness pressed into his hand and looked down to see a thin silver ring.

'Wear this,' Firella ordered. 'It's so we can find you if we get separated.' Ethan hesitatingly took it, grasping it in his palm.

The group had now all stood up, watching as the Nuns approached. The leading Nun may have been Sister Charity, although they all looked so similar that Ethan was unsure. She addressed him directly.

'Come with us, Ethan. We need you. Our Sisters of Darkness command.'

The sisters behind chanted, 'Come, come, come.'

Ledren and Firella stepped forward, as did Violet, her arm outstretched.

'We are from the Society of Potions and Technology,' Ledren said impressively yet calmly. 'Why do you want the boy?'

'He is needed,' the Nun repeated, glaring at Ledren as though his words did not matter.

'Needed by whom?' Firella demanded.

The Nun turned to her and smiled, her perfect white teeth shining.

'It is not your place to ask.'

What happened next was over within a second. The Nun's eyes glowed a ferocious red and an energy beam shot out, directed at close range to Firella. Just before it struck her, Firella became totally encased in a green light, which somehow seemed to protect her as the beam bounced off its target. The force of the attack however threw her backwards, and she landed heavily on the floor. Ledren reacted immediately and held both hands up towards the attackers. A similar green light erupted from his rings, forming a protective barrier between himself and the Nuns. As he moved his right hand in a circular motion, the barrier encompassed Ethan and the rest, and it dawned on Ethan that like the food trolley creatures, the Nuns were not flesh and blood.

The Nuns let loose. Red rays erupted from their eyes, focused on breaking down the barrier Ledren had created. One beam was directed at the ceiling, causing a chunk of it to come crashing down, narrowly missing Ledren and raining a shower of rubble. Ledren held his ground although obviously under strain as the Nuns' rays were absorbed into his green light.

Firella had now found her feet and joined the fight, holding her hands up to strengthen Ledren's defence. Violet fired a ray from her arm but found this would not penetrate the barrier to reach the Nuns on the other side.

The Nuns were closing in, attacking relentlessly as Ledren and Firella were slowly being forced back. Ledren shouted out to the group he was protecting.

'Get out! Leave now! Go!'

Ethan looked confusedly around him. Go where? They had Nuns surrounding them on three sides and behind them were a couch and a wall. There was nowhere to go! He then remembered the vial Camdex had given him to use in such an emergency as this and realised he could help.

Before putting any plan into action, however, Mistix had reached into his tunic and pulled out a handful of rings. More rings, Ethan thought. These ones were black and shiny like a reflection on still water under moonlight. Quickly Mistix slipped one onto everybody's fingers, and hurriedly instructed.

'Just relax and let it take you. I'll direct them to your destination.'

Ethan looked down at the ring on his finger and as he watched, a section of the ring seemed to grow. A long metal arm reached out and adhered itself to the base of the finger it clung on to. From this point, another arm then reached out, attaching itself to a point halfway up his hand. Three new arms then appeared, branching off into different directions, encompassing his wrist. Whatever this metallic substance was, it was growing at an exponentially faster rate, reaching up his arm, clinging to his skin, surrounding him. He started calling out in terror as it moved up his arm and then to his neck and head, metallic coldness reaching across his cheeks and forehead, covering his eyes so only slits of light could be seen between the strands. He saw through this gap the same thing was happening to the others as they were being swallowed alive by this living metal.

He felt the coldness reach down the other side of his body, his clothes pinched into his skin as it relentlessly covered him. He called out again before he heard a loud crack and a flash passed across his eyes.

Becoming completely disorientated, he felt the floor disappear and he tumbled sideways.

In reality, he had completely vanished; the only thing remaining was Firella's silver ring spinning in the spot where he had once stood.

CHAPTER 9

Ethan's eyes fluttered open, his head automatically jerking upwards from the dampness of the earth that had soaked into his cheek. The cold pressure of the metal which had enveloped him was now easing, and he saw the last metal strand retract back into the ring on his hand. Stumbling, he pulled himself upright and spun three hundred and sixty degrees, scouring his environment in panic, his breath coming in quickened bursts.

They were in a forest, and scattered around him were his companions, also rising from the spots they had been unceremoniously dumped, apparently disorientated like himself. He coughed and stumbled once more, before directing his shocked rage.

'What the hell was that?' he cried, shouting at Mistix who was steadying himself onto both feet.

Mistix didn't look impressed. 'That was saving your lives. No need to thank me.'

Ethan belted out an expletive, before clutching his chest. 'I couldn't breathe!'

'Well, you could,' Mistix contradicted. 'You're just not used to it.'

'It helps to take shallower breaths,' Kredax advised, straightening himself out.

The girls had gotten to their feet, disentangling themselves from their bags and flicking the dirt off their clothes.

'The brochures for those rings never mention how uncomfortable it is to use them!' Rose said, more as a fact than a complaint.

'I didn't know they were readily available to everyone,' Mistix purred suspiciously.

'Depends who you know,' Violet retorted, placing her hands on her hips. 'So how did you get them?'

Rose backed her up. 'And how did Ledren know you had them? He must have done or he wouldn't have told us to leave,' she said logically.

All eyes were on Mistix, including his brother Kredax. His usual infallible composure seemed to momentarily falter, before his confidence resurrected itself. He smiled, apparently unperturbed.

'Well,' he began, chuckling to himself, 'I suppose there's no reason why you shouldn't know.' He held his hands up as though in defeat. 'I was employed by the Society to keep an eye on Ethan until they arrived.'

Whatever Ethan expected Mistix to say, this was not it. Even Kredax looked incredulous.

'You?' he said in disbelief, stepping forward.

'Yes, me,' Mistix laughed. 'You know I'm quite clever and have a few useful skills. They use me sometimes and I was in the area.'

'So, you weren't shot by a bird when you came to the hospital?'

Mistix shrugged. 'Not really, though one looked at me very closely.'

'Why would *you* work for the Society?' Violet demanded. 'Or why would they employ you? It doesn't make sense.'

'The Society, by its own principles, will choose the best person for the job, regardless of anything else. And as for why am I doing it? Well… they do pay an awful lot of money.' He grinned. 'Next question?'

Rose stepped forward.

'Prove it!' she challenged. Mistix shrugged. 'Sure. I can contact them.' He reached into his tunic as though to pull something out.

'No!' Ethan interrupted, holding Mistix's arm. 'No. Not yet. I need to think.'

Mistix smiled. 'You really don't trust them. This is getting interesting,' he pondered. 'Do you still have the ring Firella gave you?'

Ethan shook his head. 'No, I dropped it.'

Mistix nodded. 'I can say my communicator broke during the displacement process, but I'll have to contact them eventually.' He removed his hand from his tunic. 'But for the moment, let's do it your way.'

Ethan felt relieved but at the same time he wasn't sure if he was doing the right thing. The look on Kredax's face suggested he wasn't, but his attention diverted to Mistix's hands.

'Did the Society give you your rings?'

Mistix shrugged dismissively. 'Some.'

'They are expensive,' Violet stated.

'Yes,' Mistix agreed. 'Is that why you don't have any?'

'We don't need them,' Rose retorted. 'We have our potions.'

'Yet I wonder why you need those?'

They were interrupted by a beeping sound coming from Ethan's wrist, and Jessica's face appeared in front of him, the image emanating from the device she had given him. Her face floated around haphazardly.

'Keep your arm still, dear, you'll make me dizzy,' she protested. Ethan obeyed.

'Now, where on earth have you kids got yourselves!' she exclaimed. 'You've suddenly jumped completely out of the city! I've been tracking you from your wrist-o-gram.'

'We had to escape,' Ethan explained, and detailed the events leading up to it, including the information Firella and Ledren had imparted.

Jessica was obviously worried. 'So, somebody still wants you.'

'Well, yes, the Nuns did,' Ethan agreed. Jessica shook her head.

'No. If they are automatons then they are working for somebody else. And for them to attack you out in the open like that, it means two things. One, they were desperate to stop you from going with the Society, and two, it may not have been essential to keep their purpose concealed any longer, which means that whatever plan is being developed could be just about ready to hatch. The Society needs to act quickly on this.'

'If they survived,' Violet pointed out.

'The Society consists of more than two people,' Jessica replied. 'And they can look after themselves. I used to babysit one of its members and she was always an independent little munchkin, very self-reliant. She still comes over for cake sometimes.'

Kredax interrupted. 'Jessica, have you found out any information yet about Ethan?'

'Yes, just a snippet,' she replied, adjusting her

perm. 'I managed to get some footage from an old friend in the human security force who was involved with your rescue.' She looked downwards. 'Hang on, I'll feed it through.'

Jessica's face disappeared, and she was replaced by a scene of fighting. Old buildings stood in the darkness as shots were fired, criss-crossing the night like crackling bolts of lightning. The security forces fought Ethan's kidnappers who counter attacked with equal ferocity. Explosions brought brickwork crumbling down and cries of pain cut through the sound of weaponry being discharged. Ethan stared in astonishment. People were fighting like this over him? Why would they do that? What was so special about him?

Jessica spoke. 'The security forces came across your captors quite innocently. Your kidnappers panicked and attacked them, which resulted in your kidnappers being killed so the whole situation was unexplained. It does appear however, that they were part of the underground network called the Deliverance, people who are intent on reclaiming control of society based on their…' Jessica's voice changed, and she whispered, 'evil persuasions.' She spoke normally again. 'On reviewing the fight, however, I noticed this…'

The scene zoomed in to one of the windows of the old buildings. A glint of light was reflected in one of the panes, and just for a second a man's face appeared before retreating back into the darkness.

'This particular building is not inhabited so there should not have been anybody inside. I'm thinking he may have been connected to your kidnapping, Ethan. So, if I can track him down it may give us a clue.'

The image flickered back to Jessica.

'Now you have landed yourselves in a forest not far from a town called Fate. My cousin's cousin has a nice little house there. I suggest you make your way there and have a bit of a rest. Her name is Mildred and she's already cooking up a batch of Heffer cakes and Kintar stew for when you arrive. Don't dawdle; I think you should lay low as quickly as possible. I'll send through the co-ordinates now. Any questions? No? Good, I have to go; the alarm on the oven is going off. May your twins be with you always.' Jessica disappeared, and an image of a map replaced her face. Mistix held up his hand and the map was sucked into one of the rings on his fingers.

The five youths regrouped.

'I suggest we do as she says and go to Mildred's,' Violet recommended.

'All of us could do with a rest,' Rose added. The two twins flicked their flaming hair back in perfect synchrony.

'Could the Nuns have tracked where we landed?' Ethan asked.

'You mean whoever is allied with them,' Mistix pointed out. 'No, I don't think so. Once the ring matrix has completely covered the user it projects a total wave camouflage. It becomes invisible. It should also prevent facial recognition from the birds, just in case whoever is causing the corruption is using them to search for us.'

'Great. Let's get going then,' Violet barked. 'Are

we going to use the rings to travel?'

Mistix shook his head. 'They need twenty-four hours to recharge. Use it now and you'd be scattered into little pieces.'

'Then you can you lead us, Mistix, since you have the map.'

Mistix assented, bowing his head. 'Of course.'

The group set off. Ethan noticed Mistix seemed to know where to go despite not looking at the image Jessica had sent him. He explained that the ring automatically 'pulled' him in the direction they wanted. As they walked, the group separated slightly, Mistix in the lead with Violet and Kredax behind, and then Rose and Ethan. They chatted quietly as they forged a track through the grasses and ferns of the forest floor.

'You and your sister seem almost used to what we've been through,' Ethan commented. 'None of what's happened seems to faze you.'

Rose shrugged. 'Violet's better than I am, but we are used to looking after ourselves. Our father has always been busy in the laboratory ever since we were little. A lot has happened in that time.'

'And your mother?' Ethan asked gently.

Rose looked down.

'She died when we were ten. But we coped and survived, it was a long time ago. Our life has been interesting. Our father has taught us a lot about his potions and we always keep a supply handy.' She patted her bag like an old friend.

'Your potions are amazing,' Ethan mused. 'What else do they do?'

Rose considered. 'A lot of them are defensive or protective. Violet and I make our own sometimes; we don't just get them from our father. It's sort of our hobby.'

'But other people have potions too, like the Society of Technology and… Potions?' The question sounded stupid as he asked it.

Rose laughed. 'Of course! Some of the potions the Society have were originally from our father! They do make their own, but I don't think they're as good as ours.' Ethan smiled as her confidence beamed. Such self-assurance would normally have irritated him but with Rose, somehow it didn't matter.

'I'm sorry you don't know who you are,' Rose said abruptly. 'I hope you find out and if you have a family, especially a twin…' she added.

Ethan nodded. 'Me too,' he said simply. He looked away, scouring the trees and bushes around him as though there was something of interest. 'I wonder what he'd be like,' he lamented.

Rose opened her bag and pulled out a vial. Its contents looked murky and foul. 'Watch this!' she said excitedly, deliberately changing the tone of the conversation and turned Ethan's attention to a small tree stump to her left. 'This is called an animate potion,' she explained, and poured half the vial's contents onto the top of the stump. Like the potion that had been applied to Ethan's wound, it seemed to take on a life of its own, spreading over the wooden surface and seeping into the cracks and crevices. The liquid changed colour, turning a phosphorous green as the volume of liquid increased and bubbled, running down the sides of the stump. Ethan watched in amazement as the whole stump base suddenly glowed and began to move. It rocked from side to side, slowly and slightly at first before gaining momentum. A root from the stump laboriously pulled itself out of the ground, spraying dirt in the air. Gaining traction, the exposed root then heaved the rest of the base out of the ground, three more roots breaking the soil surface. Like a lost puppy searching for its master, it turned in a circle before bounding up to Rose's feet, two roots clambering up onto her legs. She jumped backwards.

'Easy, Stumpy!' she exclaimed. 'You're no light-weight!'

The stump retreated, cowering like a dog that had been told off.

Ethan stood with his mouth open. 'The tree is moving,' he said unnecessarily.

'Yes, though they tend to be a bit clingy. When an inanimate object is animated, they tend to follow you around until the potion wears off. It's quite fun.'

Ethan let out a huge breath. 'I bet! That's… quite bizarre.'

Rose laughed and bent down. 'Who's a good Stumpy then.' She gave it a pat.

Ethan's head suddenly jerked to the side, aware of a rustle in the bushes to his right. Straining, he thought he saw something briefly appear above some foliage; something white and fluffy.

'Rose,' Ethan said slowly, turning. 'The Snake-shifts. Where do they usually live?'

Rose's eyes widened, also hearing rustling. She

took a breath.

'In the forests…'

They stared at each other, both thinking the same thought.

'I think we should catch up to the others,' Ethan said, but Rose was already moving.

Together, they set off in a run after the other three, Stumpy galloping along behind them kicking chunks of soil and foliage off its roots as it scuttled along.

Their companions had already stopped, waiting for them to catch up. Violet peered around them, staring at the tree trunk.

'You animated wood?' she said judgingly.

'Never mind that!' Rose huffed. 'We think there's a Snake-shift back there in the bushes.'

'Today just gets better and better, doesn't it,' Mistix said drily. 'Let's hope you haven't annoyed it.'

Rose smiled sweetly, 'Now what could we possibly do to annoy a cute little ball of fluff like that?'

'Breathe?' Kredax suggested, looking back over her shoulder.

'Let's get out of here!' Violet said warily.

They all set off, Stumpy included. As they tramped through the knee-high grass, Rose suddenly let out a shriek and literally jumped into the air, clearing Ethan's head and landing a good five metres away. To the left of where she had been stood two Snake-shifts, partly covered by a section of bush. Everyone froze, unsure as to their intention, and Violet's arm automatically pointed at the potential threat.

A strange high-pitched sound came out of the

creatures, and in unison they started jumping up and down, their soft fur fanning Ethan who stood closest. It took him a few seconds to understand.

'Are they copying Rose?' he asked incredulously.

As they listened, the sound they were making was similar to the shriek she had just uttered, and they were jumping as she had done. They then stopped and uttered another more continuous high-pitched sound.

'I think they're laughing,' Kredax observed.

'I don't find them funny,' Violet growled. 'Let's keep going.'

Cautiously they moved forward, but each step they took, the Snake-shifts bounded towards them. One took an extra leap and affectionately nuzzled itself under Kredax's arm, who found himself patting its head. The creature purred in response, green eyes gazing up at him.

'They're cute in this form,' he observed nervously.

The other Snake-shift jumped over to Violet, nudging her arm as though wishing to be patted. She reluctantly did so just so that it would stop annoying her. Its fur was soft, and she did not find it unpleasant.

'At least it keeps them happy,' she commented grudgingly.

There was further rustling in the bushes and two more Snake-shifts jumped out, with another behind them, presumably the one Ethan and Rose had heard earlier. Within seconds the group was being frantically nudged, surrounded by a rustling mass of white fur. Despite being in their friendly form, the danger the group felt was very real, and Ethan was only too aware of his recent encounter with one.

Stumpy was floundering around Rose's feet, trying to get in between her and the closest Snake-shift as though competing for affection. The situation felt like it could only end badly.

'Keep moving,' Violet advised. 'There's too many of them. If they turn, we'll be in big trouble.'

'You could use your arm on them,' Mistix suggested. 'Sort them out before things get ugly.'

'That's not an option, Mistix,' Kredax said succinctly. Mistix glared but said nothing. Ethan was half tempted to agree with Mistix.

The group's attempt to move forward was met with limited success, as the Snake-shifts did not give up. Their persistence for affection was equally matched by the teenagers' desire to escape them, though intuitively everyone suspected that if they ran, the Snake-shifts wouldn't like it. Rose half-heartedly patted the head of the one nuzzling her arm.

'Why do they like to be patted so much?' she said through gritted teeth.

Kredax replied, 'Because no one would go anywhere near them if they had the choice. And they haven't got any arms. They can't even touch each other. Even creatures need some physical contact sometimes.'

'Oh please!' Mistix jeered. 'Give them a hug if that's what you think.'

Violet was peering closely at the creature next to her.

'There could be another reason,' she said with revulsion. 'I can see little black insects on them. Maybe they just want us to scratch them because they're itchy!'

'Let them itch,' Ethan muttered dispassionately.

'Gross!' Rose cried and held her hand against her Snake-shift so that it couldn't get too close. 'We have to run for it and hope they won't follow. Violet and I can get some potions ready in case they change into something nasty. Mistix, have you got any tricks on those fingers of yours?'

'I can project a barrier the same way Ledren did at the hospital. If we can all get ahead of them, I can temporarily hold them back.'

'What range has it got?' Violet asked.

'About ten metres.'

'It's not enough. Once you create the barrier Rose and I can throw a freezing potion on it. That should maintain it, so you can get away.'

'Sounds like a plan,' Mistix agreed.

'Everyone ready to run?' Violet asked. The group assented.

'Run!' Violet called and set off in a sprint. The sudden movement gave the group the advantage, surprising the Snake-shifts who were left behind. As soon as the teenagers were clear of the jumping creatures, Mistix turned and focused his ring on them, projecting a barrier which encompassed them completely. The two girls also turned, hurling a vial each at the pulsating, green projection. The vials shattered, splattering potion across the outside and creating an immediate effect. The barrier crystallised and hardened, but more importantly became a solid entity, no longer dependent on the power emanating from Mistix's ring. Inside, the Snake-shifts became noticeably more agitated, acutely angry at having been imprisoned. Like heated up popcorn, one by one they exploded, the rat-like creatures bursting into existence, scratching menacingly at the inside wall of their enclosure.

'That's got 'em,' Mistix shouted victoriously.

'But for how long?' Kredax warned, slightly ahead with Ethan.

'Who cares, we are not waiting!' Violet exclaimed.

The teenagers ran, tearing through the forest, their senses heightened in case they were being followed or if new threats emerged. Ethan noticed Rose initially taking the lead, her robotic legs effortlessly striding in front of them, yet puffing as her arms moved in unison. She then held back, and momentarily took Ethan's hand, as though encouraging him along. Ethan felt his cheeks blush slightly, and not just because he was quickly becoming out of breath.

Mistix, Kredax and Violet lapped up the exercise as though this was nothing unusual for them.

They ran for another ten minutes, their progress eventually abruptly stopped by a criss-crossed fence encircling the edge of the forest as far as they could see. Beyond it they could see houses. The fence was green in colour, made of a material that resembled a metallic plastic and stood approximately four metres high.

'To keep the Snake-shifters in!' Violet stated, as she studied it intently.

'And us,' Ethan said forlornly.

'It shouldn't be a problem,' Rose said confidently. 'I can jump this. I can take you all over one at a time on my back.'

Violet was in no mood for delays.

'Take me first, then Ethan. I can protect him on the other side.'

Ethan raised an eyebrow. It was nice to have friends so eager to protect him and yet he still had to wonder why they were willing to do so. He now knew Mistix had a motive, but what about the girls? A sense of duty? Because they liked him? He just wasn't sure.

Violet climbed onto Rose's back, clinging to her like a sea limpet on a rock. Rose crouched down then effortlessly took off, springing high into the air, over the top of the fence and then down to the ground on the other side, wobbling slightly as she landed. Violet climbed off and Rose quickly made the jump back.

It was now Ethan's turn. He was only just taller than Rose but heavier than Violet. He tentatively put his arms around Rose's shoulders and linked them at the front, before allowing his weight to fall onto her. She didn't hesitate, crouching down once more. Ethan could feel the power of her legs as they left the earth. His own legs entwined her as they easily cleared the fence top and made the gut-wrenching plummet downwards. Rose absorbed most of the impact as they completed the jump, and Ethan casually climbed off her.

The process was repeated with Kredax, although it looked considerably more awkward as his larger frame draped off Rose like a cloak, his legs completely wrapping around her hips. Her legs held strong but her top half struggled under his weight. Nevertheless, they successfully made the jump, only momentarily losing balance as Kredax slipped off her back at the last moment.

Turning back to Mistix, Rose saw that he was now looking behind him, and it quickly became apparent why. The Snake-shifts were coming. Five of them, scrambling across the terrain, nattering to themselves with screeches and growls as a mixture of different forms of the creatures headed towards them. The rat-like abominations reached out with their three arms, while the ones with black shiny heads bared their sharpened teeth.

Rose crouched and jumped back over, landing behind Mistix. The creatures were getting closer.

'Get on!' she screamed, turning her back to him. Mistix ignored her and held up his hand. A bolt of lightning shot forth from one of his rings, searing through the air and ferociously cutting down the nearest Snake-shift. Then another bolt and a second Snake-shift fell.

'Wait!' Kredax called. 'Stop it!'

Mistix ignored him. Two more bolts and two more Snake-shifts fell, leaving just one alive. Seeing what had happened to its fellow creatures, the remaining one transformed into its final form, angry and frightening as it slithered towards them. Mistix knew his attack would not have the same effect on its toughened hide and hurled himself around Rose's neck.

Panicked, she jumped upwards haphazardly, clipping the top of the fence with her feet, throwing off their balance. The two separated in mid-air, Mistix's arm pulling Rose's head backwards as they fell. She tried to turn, ducking her head down and forcing her legs to twist and stay beneath her. Miraculously, her legs hit the ground first before falling onto her front. Mistix, on the other hand, landed on his feet and rolled to the side, cushioning the impact and jumping back upright. It was done so expertly that there was no surprise he now stood injury free.

The others rushed to Rose, who gave a groan on the ground.

'Rose!' Violet shrieked, turning her over.

'I'm okay,' she panted, groaning once more. 'I'm just bruised.'

The Snake-shift momentarily took their attention, as it pushed itself against the fence and hissed ferociously. Two of the tendrils on its stomach slithered through the gaps in the fence and reached towards Rose. She screamed and scuttled away, only just getting out of its reach in time. Stumpy placed itself between the Snake-shift and fence, apparently trying to hold back the creature, but then suddenly froze solid and tipped over. The potion had worn off, becoming wood once more.

Violet helped Rose up and the twins turned on Mistix.

'You nearly got her killed!' Violet yelled.

'That wasn't necessary!' Rose attacked, motioning to the slaughter on the other side of the fence. 'I could have gotten you out in time!'

'I didn't want to risk it!' Mistix counter attacked. 'Those things are capable of anything and they move fast. Our odds were better with four dead!'

'You just wanted to kill them!' Rose replied.

'Well, what if I did?' Mistix said slyly. 'Should that surprise you?' He shook his head. 'I needed to get rid of them before they turned into their final shape. We wouldn't have survived facing five of them!'

'We would've got out before they got to us!' Rose repeated, rubbing her sore shoulder.

'It's done now, and I'm bored talking about it.' Mistix gave her a filthy look and motioned to leave.

'You should find somewhere else to go,' Violet said suddenly, eyes pointed directly at him.

Mistix stopped and turned slightly.

'I'm here to keep Ethan safe or the Society doesn't pay me. Wherever he goes, I go.' He then looked at Violet. 'Unless you're going to fight me? Even with your potions I wouldn't recommend it.' There was an unmistakable warning in his tone. Violet said nothing. Ethan knew it wasn't because she was afraid of him, but because it wasn't worth the energy. Stalemate. For the moment.

He smiled and held up his hand full of rings. 'And I've got the map. So, let's just all get along, shall we?' He started walking. Kredax remained uncomfortably silent, and without looking up from the ground, followed his brother. Reluctantly, Ethan's party stayed at five.

The Snake-shift remained confined to the other side of the fence, hissing angrily as it watched them leave.

CHAPTER 10

The air was heavy and cold, a consequence of poor ventilation and too little movement. This was a room hidden away, squandered for private use and deliberately camouflaged. The entrance on the outside looked no different from the wall around it, a technological shield blending it into the surrounding environment. But inside was a room like no other. Not because the equipment inside would be unrecognisable to all, but because the intent inside this room was to change a world.

Two figures shuffled around a central machine, a scientific monolith reaching up towards the elevated ceiling. The base housed an array of components, carefully constructed and arranged to integrate seamlessly to form one, and protected by an opaque material like glass, but many times stronger. Above this rose a column, glowing with blackness, a cylindrical void which repelled all light and towered over the two who worked on its inner core below. The unmistakable outline of Syntax's head contrasted with the youthful woman next to him. She was lithe with a full head of curly, jet-black hair which bounced around her neck and shoulders, and was partly held in place with a large, red bow. Her face was small and pretty, matching her waif-like yet sinewy figure, which was revealed by her loosely cut black lace top and short, red, billowing skirt. She looked like a dressed-up doll, perfectly manicured with everything in place. The only thing out of place was a slight downturn of the corners of her mouth; subtle, yet some may think cruel.

'The boy has disappeared,' Carrie Jingles said disapprovingly. Her voice floated light and girl-like yet portrayed hidden menace.

'It doesn't matter,' Syntax said gruffly. 'Once the space chip activator is repaired, he can be anywhere. At least the Society doesn't have him; they may have been able to interfere.'

'He came to *you*,' she said quietly. 'It was an opportunity.'

Syntax huffed. 'Not while my brother was there, and I'm not going to look after the boy until he's needed.'

Jingles persisted. 'It's one stuff-up after another. We've let him go twice! If Mr. Jingles were still alive, he wouldn't be happy.' She pouted.

'Perhaps you shouldn't have poisoned him then,' Syntax chuckled.

'That was an accident,' she said demurely. 'I just wanted to put him to sleep for a day or two. He ate more than I thought he would. He always was a bit of a piggy though.'

'Piggy or not, it's slowed us down,' Syntax sneered. 'I want to finish this!'

'And I want to go out shopping without having to run into all those happy, good people. I need something to cheer me up.' She clasped her hands hungrily. 'Let's activate the Time Leeches now.'

'No. Everything has to be done at the same time. We'll have more chance of success with the confusion it will cause.'

'There had better be more than confusion. I want to see the population halved in time for the monthly sales.' Jingles smiled sweetly. 'And it'll be my birthday!' She tapped on the opaque covering surrounding Syntax's new brain as he bent over, staring into it. 'What are you thinking of getting me?'

Syntax glared up at her. 'Touch that again and you'll be joining your husband.'

Jingles sighed. 'Yeah, right! We need each other. Our technological skills work well together. And our aims are mutual, so you're stuck with me, like I'm stuck with you.' She checked her red bow was in place. 'What about your brother, does he suspect anything?'

Syntax huffed. 'He's too busy talking about cheese. He doesn't even know about this room despite its location.'

'Don't underestimate him. He's…'

'He's *my* brother!' Syntax interrupted. 'And not your concern!'

'He'll be my concern if I have to blow him up,' she said dreamily, smiling at the thought. 'But let's not think about the good times ahead, not yet.'

'When the birds and Leeches are activated, the slaughter will be something never seen before on this planet. But to use this first…' He held up the sphere he had shown earlier in the laboratory. 'The pandemonium will be stimulating, if only briefly. A final liberation.' He placed the sphere in an alcove within the base of their creation. 'I want the space chip activator repaired by this time tomorrow.' He turned to Jingles, hardened. 'And then it begins!'

CHAPTER II

The teenagers had been walking for an hour, mostly in silence. There was now a distinct sense of loss of cohesion between them. The girls were obviously unhappy with Mistix, who with his arrogance had shown no sign of recognizing their distrust. Kredax's silence also appeared to alienate him from the girls, while Ethan felt somehow in the middle. Not because he was on Mistix's side, but more so because he had nothing against Kredax.

They had passed through the streets of the small town. There were no high-rise buildings here, just smaller dwellings suitable for families. At nearly every corner there were monitors; a lizard on the wall, a cat on a roof, their electronic eyes seeing all. Fewer birds patrolled the sky, but nevertheless they were still present. Ethan couldn't help but ponder on the thought of who controlled them; if it wasn't the Society, then who?

Up ahead, several birds were circling at the far end of the road. The teenagers could hear a disturbance of some kind, voices shouting down a side alley. One bird flew down closer to the ground and fired, silencing the noise from whoever had been the target. The group stopped, unsure as to whether the bird was performing its duty in keeping social control or was randomly killing.

'We can go down this way,' Mistix said calmly, and led them off to a different direction. Furtively, everyone followed.

Their trek ended in front of a grand-looking house set at the end of a street. Three floors high, it had well-manicured lawns at the front and trees either side, almost the mirror image of each other. A white fence surrounded it, encapsulating a peaceful suburban home.

They approached the gate at the front. As Mistix reached to open it, he found his hand struck an invisible barrier, preventing him from opening the latch. The image of a face appeared in front of them, apparently studying the intruders. She was a woman in her fifties, with long, grey pig tails hanging down either side of her head and a fringe straight across her forehead.

'Who is it?' she asked politely, looking from one to the other.

'We were sent from Jessica,' Violet replied. 'Are you Mildred?'

Mildred smiled. 'Yes, of course. Come in.'

The gate swung open and they found they could now move forward, taking the steps up to the front door. This door also opened of its own accord, and in single file they ventured inside.

They had entered a living room, two couches at right angles to each other taking centre spot, with several armchairs randomly placed beside them. Bookcases almost completely covered each wall, making the room feel more like a library, if an unruly one. The books had been shoved onto the shelving with complete disregard to order. It wasn't this which took the newcomers' attention, however. It was the five pairs of unblinking eyes staring at them. Cats lay across the furniture, their black and white heads raised to see who had entered their domain. Panther-like, one effortlessly glided off the couch and with abnormal speed darted across the room to nuzzle Rose's leg. It made a purring sound which had a faint electronic twang to it, all the while staring at her intently. There was something unnerving about it, and Ethan realised they were robots.

Mildred burst into the room, her pigtails flying and a huge smile on her face. She was a large lady, dressed in a red check shirt and blue pants, and strangely balancing on a pair of blue high heels, perhaps trying to make an effort while having visitors. She tottered over to them, arms outstretched and apparently delighted to see them.

'Welcome, welcome! Any friends of Jess are very welcome in my house!' She gave each of them a hug in turn. Mistix grimaced.

'Actually, we only just met Jessica,' Ethan confessed. 'She's working for me.'

Mildred stopped. 'Oh. Okay then. Right.' She seemed to think it over before breaking out into another big smile. 'That's okay, buddy! We're going to become great friends anyway!' She gestured to them all. 'Come into the kitchen, I've got your food all prepared. You must be starving. Jess said you've had a hard night!'

Ethan had to agree it wasn't the best. They followed her into the next room, surrounded by the cats, which had all jumped off the furniture and now walked silently at their feet, brushing themselves up against their legs. Ethan knelt down and stroked one.

Its fur was soft, but the skin underneath felt leathery and cold. He retracted his hand.

The kitchen was densely packed with pots, pans and cooking utensils scattered across the bench-tops and hanging from various hooks. In one corner sat a strange looking white triangular structure, about the height of a man and a metre wide at the base. The surface was smooth except for a square metallic plate in the centre.

In front of them was a large, rectangular table, six places set with a plate of steaming food. Mildred heartily told them to take a seat, which they did.

The five cats now congregated at Mildred's feet, staring up as though trying to convey some message. She reached into her top pocket and pulled out a handful of small pellets.

'Here you go, matey's. Have some nice energy pellets to keep you going. Don't want you seizing up on the furniture, do we?' She scattered the pellets in front of the cats, who lapped up a couple each. One cat looked towards Ethan. Its eyes glowed brightly and hauntingly as though a ghostly spirit had entered its soul. Its pupils became pure light as the pellet re-energised its power cells before slowly subsiding to black.

Moving as one, having finished their meal, the cats turned and raced back to their positions in the lounge, sentries at the door. Ethan was unnerved by them; they were cat-like in their movements yet unnatural to watch.

Mildred took a seat and surveyed her visitors with thorough enjoyment.

'Start eating, everyone, don't be shy.' Ethan noted that Mistix had already begun eating, which didn't surprise him, but Ethan didn't need to be told twice either. He was starving and dug deep into the dish with his spoon; there was no plate technology here. The stew had a faint green tinge to it, and an aroma that he did not recognise. The taste, however, was remarkable and completely delicious.

'We can get to know each other as we eat,' Mildred said brightly, obviously eager to chat. Kredax introduced everyone, and Mildred excitedly waved at each of them in turn while saying hello. She was so bubbly Ethan liked her immediately.

'And Jessica told me your story, Ethan. I hope you don't mind,' she gushed with apology. 'It's just so strange, but it got me thinking and trying to join up all the pieces. Killer birds! Time Leeches! Space chips! And then you, Ethan! Somebody wanted those Nuns to capture you, but why? You must have something they want. Is it knowledge? Do you know something?'

Ethan shrugged. 'I don't know. I have no memory. There's nothing I could tell anybody.' He sounded dejected.

'Then have you got something on you? Do you carry something around with you? A ring, a trinket, a potion, anything?'

Ethan felt inside his front pockets. His fingers glided over three vials; two which had been given to him by Camdex and the sleeping potion from Sebastian. He also had the jewels from the Snake-shift bar. But these were given to him after he had been kidnapped, so it couldn't be these. He checked his back pockets and jacket; there was nothing else. He shook his head. Mildred looked bemused.

Violet spoke. 'There could be another reason.' She held everyone's attention. 'Maybe he did know something about the birds and Leeches, and that was why his memory was wiped somehow. But whoever is after him doesn't know he can't remember.' This seemed plausible.

Rose added, 'Or could they know how to reverse his memory loss to get the information?'

Ethan scowled. 'But what could I possibly know? I'm a teenager! There's nothing special about me!'

Mildred made a doubtful face, her rosy cheeks rounded. 'Well, I would say there is something very special about you, we just don't know what it is yet. But it seems to me that whoever is after you, they don't want to...' she gave a cough while she considered her next words '...harm you, or they could have done that already; which is *good*.' She smiled encouragingly.

Ethan sighed and suddenly felt very tired. He dug into his stew, for the moment not wishing to think about anything else but the taste in his mouth.

Rose had also decided on a change of topic.

'Do you live here by yourself, Mildred?' she asked.

Mildred looked surprised. 'I'm not here by myself, pumpkin, I have my cats! The little blighters can be quite a handful but they're a hoot to have around. Are you a cat person?'

Rose shivered, perhaps remembering the Snake-shifts. 'I've gone off furry creatures lately but I'm sure your cats are nice.'

'Well, that's okay, they say people are either cat people or wolfdog people, so who am I to judge?' Mildred suddenly gave an exclamation. 'I forgot to ask, does anybody want some salt or cat leaf clippings in their stew? Does it need more flavour?'

Everybody shook their heads, except Mistix who spoke up.

'Yes, I'd like some salt.' He seemed to be playing with the food as though unhappy with it.

'Great!' Mildred said fervently. 'I want to try out my new automatic rotating salt dispenser. I like my gadgets.' She reached over to the shelf behind her and chose a small black orb, no bigger than the palm of her hand. 'So, I press here to get it started, and then adjust the speed with this…' She manipulated the orb, and they heard a buzzing sound from across the kitchen. Towards them flew a cylindrical salt shaker with a white glow underneath, presumably the source of its propulsion. The shaker moved haphazardly across the room, flying up and down and sideways in its attempt to get to Mistix. It flew over Kredax, causing him to duck, before hovering uncertainly over Mistix's plate. Mistix leaned backwards, unsure as to what to make of this device.

'And then I press this to release the salt…'

The shaker then started to spin, flecks of salt streaming out of it. The trouble was it wasn't just going into the stew, but across the table and into Mistix's face. He spluttered and knocked it to one side. As it moved to the right, a cat suddenly pounced from the floor and chomped its mouth around it. They heard the ceramic crack as it was easily crushed in the cat's electronic jaws, salt pouring through the wiry whiskers to the floor. For a second the cat's soulless, metallic eyes seemed to flicker enjoyment, before the robot turned and slinked back to its robotic family. Mildred gave a cry.

'Blacky, you naughty cat! You're not being let out tonight!' Mildred's pigtails seemed to swing with annoyance. 'Well, that wasn't supposed to happen. S'pose I better clean up the mess now!' She clapped twice and shouted randomly: 'Cleaner! Code white in the kitchen!'

This time the group heard a high-pitched whirring noise and a UFO-like object flew in from the living area. After scanning the area, it hovered over the shattered remains of the salt shaker and in one impressive display of suctioning power, inhaled the debris. Spinning around, it quickly returned to where it had come from.

'That cleaner is one of my favourite gadgets. The cats are hard to toilet train and they leave pellets all over the house, so this sucks them up and recharges them all at the same time. It actually came with the cats, sort of a 'buy five cats and get one free flying cleaner' deal.' Mildred finished the last of her stew, having inhaled it in much the same manner as her cleaner had inhaled the salt shaker.

'Mildred,' Kredax said, 'I was wondering if you remember much about when the birds first appeared?' He placed his spoon down, also having finished his meal.

'The birds?' Mildred looked thoughtful. 'Well, I

was very young at the time, but I remember the first time I saw one.' Her mood became more sombre and she let out a sigh.

'It was a very tricky time. Difficult and disruptive children had now become violent and murderous adults. People were afraid to leave their houses and even that wasn't safe, as people were randomly attacked in their own homes. Weapons were everywhere as they were needed for protection, but it only ended up with more killing. Transport was breaking down, stores were getting robbed and burnt down, fires were popping up everywhere around the cities, food supply was threatened. Many people feared going to work. My parents were no different and didn't have a lot of money, so they had to keep working. I remember how protective they were, scared to leave me alone and I was never allowed outside unless they were with me. One day, though, I was so fed up being stuck inside I crept out the back door, just to get some air for five minutes. There was a path from our place which led into the forest, so I thought I'd have a quick walk and come back before my parents noticed I'd gone.'

'What about the Snake-shifts?' Ethan asked.

Mildred shook her head. 'There were no Snake-shifts back then. They were unheard of. They were the result of animal experimentation, or at least that's the theory. They may have been deliberately created, of course, but nobody really knows. There have been a lot of creatures produced by potion manipulation in the last fifty years. Most of them you wouldn't want to meet in a dark alley, I can tell you!' Mildred took a breath and continued. 'So, I walked into the forest, but I'd only taken a few steps in when I heard someone crying out. Further down at the forest edge two men were attacking a third. They were being… really violent, which shocked me, and probably only to steal a few Trons. But as I watched, I saw this bird fly in from over my house, straight for the men. The bird fired twice, and the two attackers fell. The other man dragged himself off the ground and stumbled away. I was petrified and ran straight back to the house, not understanding what had just happened. But after that day, more and more birds were appearing and began policing the streets. The Society of Technology and Potions were also newly formed back then and had informed the public that together with the birds, they were there to keep order and to make sure the violence stopped. It took a while before people got the message, but eventually everything settled down and people could start having a normal life again. There was a lot of resentment though, and still is; I'm surprised there haven't been attacks on the Society, although they *are* quite powerful now and have many members. They have a huge variety of strong potions and use many types of rings. The birds are only one defence.'

'The birds aren't theirs,' Ethan said abruptly. 'Ledren told me that. The Society doesn't know who controls them.'

Mildred was obviously surprised, and then spoke thoughtfully.

'There were rumours, of course, that the Society had nothing to do with them, and lots of alternative theories as to where they had come from, but most people didn't actually believe them. I've probably even got a book or two on the subject, somewhere.'

Ethan was interested.

'Could I see one?' he asked hopefully.

Mildred nodded. 'Sure, if I can find it. We can have a look now if you've all finished your meal?'

They had, so Mildred got up and led them into another room, off the kitchen. The group was astonished to find that this room, too, was wall to wall books.

'Why do you have so many?' Mistix asked, unimpressed.

'It's a lost form of art!' Mildred answered emphatically. 'Everybody reads electronically or virtually with their projection chips, but you can't touch it, you can't smell it, you can't feel the history. Each book is a link to the past! And it can show us where *not* to go in the future.'

Mistix looked sorry that he'd asked.

Ethan perused the spine of some of the books on the shelf in front of him: *Safety Comes First – Using Gadgets in a Modern Society; How to Ensure Your Gadgets Aren't Watching You – A Beginner's Guide; My Gadget, Your Gadget – Whose is the Best?*

Mildred obviously did like her gadgets. The next book on the shelf was different: *Romeo and Juliet* by William Shakespeare. It looked very old. Ethan shrugged; probably some unknown writer.

Mildred was running her fingers along the spines of the books, talking to herself as she read each one. Eventually she gave a hoot and pulled one off the shelf.

'Here we go! *An A-to-Z Guide of Unsubstantiated Theories*. Just what we want!' She opened the book on a small table beside her and fished through the pages.

'Theories on angels… birds… no not that kind of bird… aha! The bird we want!'

The group crowded around. Mildred was reading ahead.

'There seems to be several theories on where the birds came from. The accepted theory is that they were released from the Society of Technology and Potions, but the Society has often been non-committal on the subject, causing speculation about whether they had anything to do with it. Two other main theories stand. Firstly, a religious order called the Sisters of the Living, are believed to have been involved. Their convent is one of the first known sightings of the birds. The origins of the Nuns themselves are unclear, but it is thought that they have access to, or possess, sophisticated technology which enabled them to create the birds as a focus of good. The convent itself is never open to outsiders, and the Nuns have never made public comment on the subject.' Mildred turned the page. 'The second theory is that they were created by a scientist who had been intent on controlling the world, but somehow the birds became completely independent, or perhaps the scientist had died, so that they functioned autonomously and on-going. The birds have, at times, made reference to a creator, but will not specify who the creator was. Or indeed, if there was more than one.'

Ethan remembered back to when he had first met

Budgie. He had mentioned his creator, but Ethan hadn't thought to ask who that may be.

Mildred continued. 'The other mystery concerning these birds is whether they require maintenance, and if so, who is maintaining them? Sophisticated tracking devices have been employed to follow them, but the birds emit a cloaking signal which, up to now, has been impossible to counter. Attempts at capturing one to dissect have also been unsuccessful, as not only do they have significant fire power, but if captured whereby there is no likelihood of escape, they have shown on numerous instances to have a self-destruct mechanism. Since the first time they appeared in our skies, nobody has ever managed to pull one apart to determine how they are constructed.'

Mildred looked up. 'Fascinating, isn't it? We have lived with them for years, but nobody knows anything about them.'

It was a sobering thought, as though nobody had ever thought about it before. Ethan felt bleak. 'And now they are starting to kill people…'

CHAPTER 12

After serving Heffer cakes, Mildred directed the teenagers to the upstairs bedrooms. Although now it was early evening, everyone was exhausted from recent events and were led willingly to their places of rest. Ethan had his own room, while Mistix and Kredax shared another opposite to his, and the girls were further down the hall.

Ethan's room had a double bed, a built-in wardrobe (which opened automatically when you asked it to) and various dolls and stuffed animals placed on a small shelf to the left of the wardrobe. Ethan barely even noticed them, and collapsed onto his bed, his mind whirling both from tiredness and confusion as to what was going on. Try as he might, he still couldn't come up with a reason why the Nuns, or whoever were controlling them, would want him. His memory was just as foggy; nothing was returning to him.

He closed his eyes to encourage sleep but gave a small start as he heard his bedroom door click open. Standing in the gap was Mistix, his figure silhouetted against the brighter light of the hallway. Without waiting for an invitation, he slipped inside and closed the door, looking at Ethan all the while. Ethan sat up, suddenly tense.

'What do you want?' he asked.

Mistix frowned. 'Nothing, I just want to talk to you.'

Ethan relaxed slightly. 'Okay,' he said warily, and waited.

Mistix took a step closer.

'I just wanted to know what you think about the girls.'

It was Ethan's turn to frown. 'The girls? Why?' Ethan felt his guard go up and realised that subconsciously he had become protective of them.

'Don't you think it's strange that they are here with us? They could just go home. They don't know you, they only just met you, but they are putting themselves in danger just by being near you.'

Ethan squirmed, as Mistix was verbalising what he himself had wondered.

'Well, you're still here,' Ethan retorted.

Mistix gave one of his forced smiles. 'But I've got a reason to be here; a very good reason.'

'Well, maybe someone's paying *them,*' Ethan said sarcastically.

'Exactly,' Mistix replied bluntly. Silence followed. Mistix looked in deadly earnest and Ethan sat with his mouth open. Mistix was serious, and Ethan didn't know what to say.

'That's...' He wanted to say *'not true'* but the words would not form on his lips. His mouth closed.

'It makes sense,' Mistix continued. 'There's something special about you but only to those who know what it is. No offence,' he added smoothly.

Ethan stared. 'Violet saved me from the Nuns, she just happened to be there. It was co-incidence that they got involved.'

Mistix looked at him, like a parent to a foolish child.

'I don't believe in co-incidences, I'm not so naive.

There's a reason they are here, and I don't believe in their *we can be whoever we like, it's a choice* crap. One of them is not who they pretend to be, and both have a hidden motive. You need to wake up.'

Ethan looked annoyed. 'And I'm supposed to believe what *you* say?' he said challengingly.

'Of course, I'm looking out for your best interests…'

'…or you don't get paid,' Ethan said mockingly.

'Reason or not I'm here to protect you. And there's more to it than that if you use your brain.'

Ethan went red. 'Like what?' he snapped.

Mistix behaved like he had the upper hand and was closing in for the kill. 'The fire power from Violet and the Nuns, of course!' He waited, as though there was something obviously wrong with what he had said. Ethan didn't know what he meant. A knock on the door broke the tension, and it slowly opened.

'Everything okay?' Violet asked inquisitively, glancing from one boy to the other. Mistix reacted quickly.

'All good. Just having a quick chat. Time to sleep anyway.'

Taking one last look at Ethan, he slipped past Violet and back into his own room. Violet looked inquiringly at Ethan.

'Everything's fine,' he said bashfully, almost ashamed at the conversation he had just had. 'Goodnight, Violet.' He gave her a half smile.

'Goodnight. May your twin…' She stopped herself, looked embarrassed and softly closed the door.

Ethan leant back onto his bed, now more awake than ever. Did Violet hear their conversation? What did Mistix mean about the fire power? What was strange about it? His mind went back to Violet firing at the Snake-shift and the Nuns, and also the Nuns firing at Ledren and Firella. He re-imagined the scenes, the Nuns' eyes blazing, Violet's arm flashing; rays from each blast slicing through the air. Sleep began washing over him, tiredness pulling his resting body into the bed beneath him. He struggled to stay focused, transfixed on Mistix's words which were slowly slipping away. His eyes closed heavily, yearning to block out the light and allow his mind to be released from reality.

His thoughts turned to dreams, and truth turned to imagination. He was now in the middle of a battle, two great armies fighting it out. A battalion of Nuns held position to his left, eyes blazing, shooting great blasts of heat in all directions. To his right was an army of Violets, all identical, arms raised, shooting mercilessly at the Nuns. He looked above and saw the sun's light being drowned out by a huge swath of birds, a massive metallic curtain blocking out the sky. They too fired, randomly cutting down Nuns and Violets alike, allowing no distinction between them. Ethan felt no threat; he was a watcher, an observer only, feeling the heat from the fire power but not in any danger.

Red rays flashed from left to right, from right to left, above to below, searing the air in front of him. His vision became narrow, eliminating peripheral vision, only seeing directly ahead, only seeing the rays of death crossing paths, almost at his fingertips. The heat, the noise, the scorching, it was all so close, and he could see it so perfectly. And then it became so clear. It was so obvious. The answer was right in front of him, and he knew what Mistix had meant. The rays were all the same. Whether from the Nuns, or the Violets, or the birds, there was no difference between the fire power. They were the same. The same technology; the same origin. They were… exactly… the same.

CHAPTER 13

In the morning Ethan lay with his eyes open, staring at the ceiling. He didn't know what to make of his new realisation. If the firing technology used by the Nuns, Violet and birds were all identical, did that mean they were all made by the same person or people; or did it just mean the technology was obtained from the same source, like a manufacturer? But Violet had said her father had made her arm. And the Nuns were evil, so it could make sense that Syntax had been involved with arming them, but the birds were, until recently, a force for good. Why would Syntax arm the birds to protect good people from the bad? Or had he sold the technology to others who had then built the birds? But if that was the case, he might know who built the birds!

His mind was spinning, but Ethan couldn't help but feel he wanted to go back to the hospital and find out the answers to his questions from Syntax, although he had to admit, he wasn't sure if Syntax would answer any. He also did not know what to do with Rose and Violet. Surely, they would know something about the technology in Violet's arm, but was Mistix right? Could he trust them? He wanted to, badly, but now he just wasn't certain. Were they here with him for some other purpose that he did not know about?

He pulled himself out of bed and was surprised to see the door open once more, and even more surprised to see Mistix standing there again. Like a re-run of the night before, he closed the door and spoke.

'I've been doing some research about the guy in the building that Jess showed us,' he announced. Despite himself, Ethan was interested.

'Who is he?' he asked.

Mistix seemed pleased he had Ethan's attention.

'His name is Enoch Triton. Turns out he's a member of the Deliverance. I found out where he lives. We could pay him a visit and see what he knows.' Mistix smiled.

'How do you know where he lives?' Ethan asked suspiciously.

'I told you, I have a few useful skills. Tracking down people is just one of them.'

He raised his hand and from one of his rings there projected a multitude of images. People. Places. Addresses. Data. A constant whirlpool of information.

'I can access the four corners of this world. I can find out where people hide, who they're connected to, what their history is. I'm also trained in combat. The Society chooses their employees for good reason.'

Ethan didn't know how to respond to this boast.

The projection disappeared. 'I suggest you, me and Kredax go to this guy's place. We could leave before the girls get up. It's only a couple hours walk from here.'

'Can we use the rings yet?'

'No, they're not ready.'

Ethan was unsure. 'If this guy works for the Deliverance, he's not just going to tell us why I was kidnapped. The girls could help with their potions, and we may need protection.'

Mistix bristled and held up the rings on his fingers. 'I don't need protection and neither does Kredax. We can't trust the girls. It's better we go alone.'

Internally Ethan winced. He didn't want to have to choose between Mistix and the girls. Why didn't it surprise him that Mistix was putting him in this position?

'No,' Ethan said succinctly. 'I don't want to leave them behind.' He opened the door and turned. 'You're supposed to be protecting me anyway. Why put me in danger by taking me to this guy's home?'

Mistix said abruptly, 'You can stay here then, but I'm still going. If I can find out why they are after you, then I can protect you better.'

There was some logic to the argument. Ethan shook his head. 'No, I want to go with you. All this is because of me, I should be there.'

Mistix raised an eyebrow. 'You're so noble! I'm going to be sick.'

They heard a voice bellowing from downstairs. Mildred had prepared breakfast and was letting everybody know about it. Before long, the five visitors had indulged in a hot cooked meal. Ethan had no idea what any of it was, but he saw Mildred take the last plate from the big white triangle thing in the corner, so it appeared that this was a machine to cook food.

After breakfast, despite Mistix's viewpoint on the girls, Ethan told Rose and Violet about Mistix's investigations, without indulging that he had wanted to leave them behind. He could tell that Mistix was silently seething but he said nothing. All agreed that going to Enoch's residence could be the quickest way to find the truth as to what was going on. They told Mildred they had to go out but not where to, although she firmly suggested they stay where they were considering the circumstances. The teenagers confidently told her that they would be careful and could look after themselves, to which she put her hands on her hips and muttered how the kids these days thought they knew it all just because they had a few potions and rings! It didn't change anything though, and the group left, thanking Mildred for her hospitality and assuring her that they would see her later. Mildred reluctantly grumbled, and with some meaning said, 'May your twins be with you always.'

The day outside was harsh; a cold wind blowing through them with dark clouds rushing above. As they left and shut the gate, just for a second Ethan felt strangely perturbed, as though this day was closing in on them and they were heading towards disaster. Or was it fate? Perhaps both, but his footsteps, just for a moment, seemed slowed, trying to tell him to stop and turn around. He shrugged it off, drawing his jacket tightly around his chest with folded arms. The others also braced themselves against the weather, somehow anticipating an arduous day. At this point they were heading towards a confrontation with an unknown person, possibly a killer, without any idea of the dangers he may present. Still, at least they were doing something, and he had quiet confidence in his companions' abilities.

They forged their way against the blasts of wind, turning down a more sheltered street, which was holding a market of some kind. Birds flew above, while people hung about below, perusing the items for sale, and Ethan was immediately intrigued. Despite their mission, the travellers were drawn to look because of the numerous demonstrations by the sellers. To his left sat a girl perched tentatively on a stool and receiving a haircut, while the seller, a short and stout bald man, stood nearby. Ethan noted the girl's apparent nervousness as the haircutter was a floating gadget; a giant eye with three metallic arms attached, two of which held scissors while the third was a claw like hand which lifted and teased her hair while the scissors chopped. She giggled as a big chunk of hair fell past her face while her mother looked on. At the back of the stall there hung a number of the hair cutting gadgets eager to be sold, their scissors snapping repeatedly like crab claws.

Amused, Ethan turned to the stall opposite. This seller, an older lady dressed in bright yellow clothes, was selling a collection of gadgets which were furiously knitting a jumper. There was a different gadget creating each sleeve, while two more worked on the body of the hanging garment, which was suspended in the air over a hook while the robots buzzed around it. A small collection of onlookers watched as they worked. Glancing at it briefly, Ethan looked forwards through the crowd, and what he saw made him freeze. The crowds were parting, and through them glided a mass of Nuns. The others had also seen them, but nobody made a move. These Nuns were obviously different. They wore white instead of the black robes of those he'd encountered earlier, and the expressions of these ladies were friendly, making pleasantries to the people around them. As they approached, the closest looked straight at Ethan and smiled. Out of the corner of his eye, he saw Mistix recoil. The girls and Kredax were not in his line of sight. The Nuns paraded past, one after the other, until the final one stopped and studied Ethan. She held a hand up and touched him gently on the forehead. Even though it was cold like that of the other Nuns he'd met, he did not feel threatened.

'May you have the strength to face your endurances, and the courage to choose the correct path.' She bowed and continued on her way. Ethan turned to the others questioningly.

'They do that sometimes,' Mistix drawled. 'Don't feel special.'

'They were the Sisters of the Living!' Ethan realised. 'Weren't they?'

Kredax confirmed.

'So, they're good?'

Kredax winced at the question about their orientation. Immediately a bird flew down from above, swooping towards Ethan. Mistix rolled his eyes. For a second Ethan felt panicked, but then regained his composure, thinking fast.

'Yes, those gadgets really are good, aren't they?' he said loudly, glancing back at the stalls. 'We will have to buy some… later.' He subtly took note of the bird's position, wondering if it believed his bluff. Its eyes spun around in its sockets, before turning and flying off. Ethan let out a relieved breath.

'They are different to the other Nuns, yes,' Rose said softly.

'Could they help us?' Ethan suggested eagerly. 'Maybe they know something about the other Nuns and why they want me?' Ethan asked this question for two reasons. Firstly, it was a valid question. Secondly, he wanted to see the girls' reaction. If they were somehow connected to the bad Nuns, they may not want him to find out anything about them. The girls' reaction was not encouraging.

'I don't think so,' Violet said. 'If they even knew who you were, they wouldn't have just walked straight past. You shouldn't advertise who and where you are.'

'But they are…' Ethan wanted to say good but stopped himself and regurgitated what Rose had said. '…different to the other Nuns. Surely they wouldn't tell them where I was.'

'It's not worth the risk. Let's stick to the plan and go to this Enoch's place.' She grinned. 'Let's kick some butt.'

So that was settled.

CHAPTER 14

Jingles was agitated. She pouted and huffed, flexing her arms and randomly toying with the electronics in front of her. Syntax had left the room, leaving her alone with their creation. He'd done this, many times before, of course, but this time Jingles had an agenda.

'You know,' she said lightly, verbalising her thoughts, 'I'm not sure we have tested our equipment properly yet.' She shook her head rapidly, her curls bouncing back and forth. 'No, I don't think so! And we need to be *really* sure everything works.' She now nodded her head, as though convincing herself. 'And what's a little bit of terror before the main event? Or pre-terror as I like to call it.' She stifled a giggle. 'It won't hurt, it might even be good for people, get them to run, to exercise, instead of playing with their stupid gadgets!' The corners of her lips turned upwards, relishing the thoughts rushing through her head. She swooped down onto the panel to her left, her hand hovering above a certain component. A holographic map appeared in front of her eyes and she ogled it intently.

'Not in the city, Jingles; that might cause too much commotion. Try a town or two just outside the main city area; some boring little backwater that nobody cares about. They might even thank me for livening up their dull stinking lives.' She pointed at a spot on the map. 'Here looks good. Boring, boring, boring! I feel bored just looking at it. Who would call their town 'Daisy' anyway? Some mad psychotic do-gooder.' She gave a shriek of delight and clasped her hands in excitement. 'Well, Daisy is about to wake up!' Her voice turned into a snarl, rising higher in pitch with expectation. 'They'll thank me in the morning!' Her pointer finger flashed out, piercing right through the map. 'And while I'm at it, I'll do this town called Fate as well!'

Ethan's group had almost made it through the throng of people at the market. The latest stall was demonstrating something called a 'refresher gadget,' which was a tiny human-like robot with a sponge cleaning attachment. It dove down underneath the shirt of a sandy haired man who had volunteered to try it. He squirmed and laughed as it gave him a hand-wash, apparently the ideal solution for those who need to freshen up and are too busy or unable to have a shower. Once it had finished, the robot jumped back out from his shirt, and flicked the sponge into a bucket onto the ground, holding its nose in disgust as it did so. The crowd laughed, and several moved forward to purchase one.

'Can we get out of this stupidity?' Mistix demanded, apparently unimpressed. Ethan had to admit they could be using their time more productively.

A cold blast suddenly ruffled his hair, and he heard the howl of the wind tear through the narrow street. He shivered and somehow the air felt different. He turned back towards the marketplace and blinked. It seemed to be growing darker, or were his eyes playing tricks on him? Was the market actually darker or were there just *patches* of darkness? There were areas that seemed to be blotting out the light. Hazy distortions of blackness were appearing everywhere. The happy ambience of the market suddenly changed and there were shrieks of alarm. Ethan felt Rose's hand on his arm as the danger became palpable. The areas of blackness were solidifying.

'Time Leeches!' Violet spat, horrified.

Directly in front of them a Leech materialised. It was roughly the size of a human, with shiny skin and circular ridges twisting around its body. The distance between each ridge changed as it elongated its repulsive shape. At the top of its form, the aberration had a vacuous mouth, and as it turned its head downwards, they could see the protruding teeth inside.

The Leech moved quickly, suckering itself onto the man who had been trying out the refresher gadget. He screamed and tried pulling away, but the edge of the Leech's mouth literally rolled over him, covering firstly his head and then devouring his entire body. His screams continued for only a few more seconds, before the noise stopped and the Leech appeared to swell, its body gorged with sustenance.

At the sight of this even Mistix appeared horror struck.

Initially shocked, Violet regained her senses and quickly raised her arm. She fired, striking a glancing blow at the base of the creature. Blood spurted out as the body deflated, shrinking in size like a balloon releasing its gas, a river of red oozing across the pavement.

The crowd had turned desperate. Some had been

too slow to escape the surprise appearance of the Leeches as they solidified; others were so shocked they had lost their wits, running in all directions only to careen head-long into each other. Violet waved her arm towards the pandemonium but could not get a clear shot at the Leeches.

The hairs on the back of Ethan's neck were raised, and he realised a Leech had materialised behind them. He spun around to see the creature no more than several metres away, expanding itself, looming higher and higher. His automatic reaction was to reach for his only protection; a vial from his pocket. Grasping one with a shaken hand, he hurled it, the fragile glass breaking on the black skin, the potion inside adhering to its target like glue. He didn't know which potion this was, so he reached for a second, but there was no need. The Leech's skin crystallized and froze, holding the creature like a repulsive statue.

Mistix had now turned and with a single well-positioned sideways kick, he shattered the structure, chunks of frozen Leech cascading to the ground, a ghastly exposé of black and red.

What happened next was a blur. Ethan became disorientated as he was engulfed in a thick green light. The world outside became obscure, separated, cut off. Panicked, he reached upwards and felt a resonating barrier around him, trapping him in the confined space. He realised it must have been created by Mistix. There were screams all around him, but his isolation formed protection. He spun around only to feel a pressure creeping up his arm and he knew what was happening even before he looked. His ring had been activated. He reached to pull it off, but it was far too late, the cold metallic arms had already reached his face and he felt the fear of suffocation once more. Struggling for breath, he saw through the green light the outline of Violet, now firing one shot after another. Ethan screamed out, but once again he was taken captive by this living metal.

Seconds later his whole world moved, and he was gone.

CHAPTER 15

He must have passed out. That was the only explanation as day was now night. Ethan was once more face down on cold earth. His head gradually cleared as he pulled himself up, and his thoughts immediately turned to his companions. Mistix was sitting on a rock, his head in his hands, recovering from the effects of the ring. But there was nobody else.

'Where are they?' Ethan croaked, his throat dry, stumbling to his feet. Mistix looked up.

'I don't know.'

Ethan reeled. 'What? How can you not know?'

Mistix sounded defensive. 'The rings were not one hundred percent charged. They've been sent somewhere else.'

'Where?'

Mistix shrugged. 'I don't know.'

Ethan was aghast.

'You said if the charge wasn't complete, they'd be scattered into little pieces!'

Mistix now seemed annoyed. 'The rings were almost completely charged. It's more likely the co-ordinates have been affected. They'll be fine.'

Another thought occurred to Ethan and the blood drained from his face.

'Did you leave them there deliberately?' The pause was longer than he would have liked.

Mistix stood up, and slowly approached Ethan. He spoke calmly and purposely.

'Whether I left them there deliberately, or the

rings sent them somewhere else, or they got up and left because they didn't want to hang around you anymore, the important thing is that they are not here. So, stop bleating and let's get going.'

Ethan's fists clenched.

'If you did it on purpose...'

'You'll what?' Mistix interrupted. 'I could snap your neck before you even realised what was happening. It's better they are not here, I told you, the girls can't be trusted.'

'Your brother was there too!'

'My brother?' Mistix seemed to contemplate, and then stated offhandedly, 'Yes, he was.' There was no indication of concern with his affirmation. The boys stared at each other, waiting for the next move. Ethan turned and sat on a rock.

'I want you to find them.'

Mistix laughed. 'I can't.'

Ethan flashed with anger.

'You said you could find out where people are; you showed me with your ring!'

'I can find people because of the tracks they leave. Electronic communications, payments, societal monitoring, correspondence, use of data, associations, visual monitors. I can't just find someone when they've been randomly transported somewhere two seconds ago.' His teeth clenched. 'Now stop wasting my time. We need to go, now!'

Ethan was furious, but he had no recourse. He wanted to get up and leave, but he knew that was not the sensible option. He didn't even know where he was. At this point, together with Jess, Mistix was still the best chance of finding out what he needed to know. But he hadn't finished yet.

'Do you enjoy it?'

Mistix looked blankly at him. 'Enjoy what?'

Ethan stepped forward. 'Being bad!' He spoke the words vehemently, deliberately taunting with the forbidden term. Mistix seemed surprised at his impudence, but had no qualms in answering.

'Yes.' He was expressionless. 'Very much!' And then he smiled.

Ethan turned away, sickened.

'Can we go now?' Mistix asked tauntingly. 'Have you finished?'

His tone became matter of fact. 'We are very close to Enoch's house. Let's do this.'

He turned to leave. Ethan hesitated, watching him walk off. But then reluctantly followed, hating himself for every step that he took in Mistix's wake.

Violet and Rose surveyed the battleground in front of them. Remnants of Leech were splattered all over the place, interspersed with bodies of people who did not make it. The fight was over relatively quickly. Seconds after Ethan and Mistix had disappeared, the birds became involved, firing succinctly from their vantage point above. The Leeches were blasted apart, exploding like smashed lumps of black and red jelly. Most of the crowd had fled, though a few remained to tend to the fallen. The girls were looking for Kredax.

'He may have used the ring,' Rose postulated.

'I don't know,' Violet replied. 'I didn't see him. I

just saw Ethan and Mistix disappear.' Her eyes flashed. 'We let them get away! We should have thought he might use the ring again!'

Rose shook her head. 'There's nothing we could have done, getting the ring off him would have been impossible.'

Violet reached down and slipped Mistix's ring off her finger.

'We should remove this, Mistix could send us off to anywhere whenever he likes.'

Rose also removed hers.

'So, what do we do now?'

Violet looked at her. 'I think we both know, don't we?'

Rose nodded slowly. 'Yes,' she agreed solemnly. 'I think we do.'

Enoch's house was old and expansive; it seemed being a member of the Deliverance had substantial benefits. Set upon a sizeable estate, the house loomed out of the darkness, partly hidden by forest-like trees, unadulterated bushes and unkempt lawns. Vines snaked haphazardly across the ground, causing Ethan to imagine hundreds of small Snake-shifts circling his feet, which did nothing to alleviate the trepidation he felt. He did, however, feel comforted by the fact that there was no sign of life. The house was in darkness and not a sound could be heard.

They had made their way to a side window. Mistix had become silent and serious, and Ethan realised that he was now at work. This was what he had been trained for, but he couldn't help but wonder… who had done the training?

Mistix touched a ring on his hand and held it in front of the window. A white beam enveloped the window and the glass literally just melted away, the liquefied substance oozing down the side of the house. Moving his hand forward a fraction, a smoky gas hissed out into the room from the same ring, quickly forming a thick fog, which spread rapidly. As the flow of gas stopped, the fog thinned out and Ethan was surprised to see silver wavy lines moving rhythmically through the air. Intrigued, he watched as Mistix flicked a catch on a particularly large ring and out flew something resembling a small fly. Its body glinted in the moonlight making Ethan believe it to be metallic. It buzzed haphazardly into the room, dodging the wavy lines as they rolled through the air and quickly made its way to the back of the room. A fierce blue beam shot out of it, targeting a section of wall that exploded in a shower of light and sparks. The wavy lines promptly disappeared. The 'fly' then flew off into an adjoining room and they heard once more a small explosion.

'I hope nobody's home to hear that,' Ethan muttered nervously.

'They're not,' Mistix answered. 'I've already checked.'

Ethan turned. 'How?'

Mistix waved his hand and a holographic image appeared in the air in front, showing rooms, corridors and stairways.

'This is a map of the house. If there was anybody here, they would show up as a red figure. As you can see, there are no red figures. We are the two blue ones.'

Ethan looked intently. The two blue figures appeared to be in the shape of animals. Although small, he could make out one was like a scaly reptile, the other a ball of fluffy fur.

'Why do we look like that?' Ethan asked.

Mistix looked intrigued. 'The ring acts as an empath; it senses our inner emotions and depicts it in the form of an animal.'

Ethan laughed. 'Well, one of us looks like a Snake-shift!'

There was no reply.

Mistix then pointed to the map with his free hand.

'There are some areas here that seem interesting. I want to check them out.' He pointed to the third floor on the opposite side to where they were.

'If Enoch isn't here then what are we looking for?' Ethan asked.

Mistix looked at him. 'Anything that may link you to him. A man of his position could leave some interesting clues.'

Ethan blinked. 'His position?'

Mistix smiled. 'Yes. He's one of the leaders of the Deliverance.'

Gritting his teeth, Ethan replied, 'You didn't tell me that.'

With a shrug, Mistix brushed it off. 'I have now. But the fact that he's a leader is a good thing. What better way to get information than going to the top?' Without another word he effortlessly lifted himself through the window frame, his feet landing silently on the other side. Feeling like a sheep following its shepherd, Ethan copied, swallowing his irritation.

They found themselves adjusting to the semi darkness. Mistix enabled a faint light to emit from yet another ring on his left hand. It was very subtle; not strong enough to be blindingly obvious to an outside observer, but strong enough to lighten the shadows.

They were in a large room and faced a wall of masks, strung up like a display of grotesque faces staring down at them. The expressions were distorted, snarling and leering with blackened gaps for eyes and deformed mouths with pointed teeth. Ethan couldn't imagine why anybody would keep a collection like this, unless they were actually worn for some reason. Could they be used by the Deliverance?

Mistix barely batted an eye at them, instead choosing to move out into the main corridor. He moved silently like a ghost, alert and poised for action. Ethan caught up and together they snuck towards a staircase ahead of them. The floor was wooden yet firm without creaks, and the corridor housed a number of paintings on the wall. From what Ethan could see, they displayed a scary collection of people; men and women with glaring eyes and threatening gestures, reaching out towards the viewer. They portrayed dominance and intimidation. Ethan was beginning to get a sense of the evil of this group, and just for a second it reminded him of the feelings he had had the first time he met Mistix; a sixth sense telling him to be wary. Having gotten to know Mistix some of the initial apprehension had waned, but he needed to remind himself that the reason for it still existed, and he should be careful.

Climbing the stairs, they found themselves in an open lounge, with multiple doorways leading off it. A scorched hole in one of the walls indicated that the 'fly' had been up here already, taking care of the alarm system. There were heads of various creatures hanging garishly above a mantel piece. One was easily recognisable as a Snake-shift, its fluffy white fur puffed out as far as it would go, its hollow eyes staring straight ahead. The mantel piece also displayed smaller creatures: a huge bug, a rodent, a number of crustaceans of some kind, all frozen to the spot. Mistix and Ethan kept going, passing the menagerie and down another corridor.

As their footsteps moved away, there was sudden movement, and bright red eyes came to life, gleaming in the gloom.

Mistix stopped at a doorway and worked quickly. He held up both hands, palms outwards. A fierce flash burst from rings on his hands and two beams converged onto the top of the door.

'The opening mechanism is hidden just below the frame. It shouldn't take long to disable it.'

Ethan felt confused. As far as he could tell the door was wooden and old, with a doorknob sitting at waist height tempting him to turn it. He reached out.

'No!' Mistix hissed. 'Touch it and you'll put me out of a job.'

Ethan withdrew his hand.

There was a small explosion at the top of the door and it slid upwards, the knob retracting into the door itself. They stood ogling the room.

There were potions everywhere, vials set in

containers on shelving which circled the room. From ground level to ceiling, there was nothing in the room except potions.

'This must be one of their potion storage areas, just a small one by their standard.' Mistix held up a warning hand. 'Don't go in, there's bound to be other surprises that I don't feel like dealing with.'

'We can't take some?' Ethan ventured.

'It's not what we came for. Although,' he added under his breath, 'it's good to know where they are.'

'They use these potions to hurt people, don't they?' Ethan asked. 'Or at least they intend to use them that way?'

Mistix couldn't care less. 'Maybe.'

'Then let's destroy them. Use your rings. Or the fly thing.'

Mistix turned to him and said enigmatically. 'No. No, I don't think I'll be doing that.'

Ethan pursed his lips and suddenly felt very stupid. To all intents and purposes, he realised Mistix was probably on their side. Just not at this moment. Of course, he wasn't going to sabotage them.

Ethan unexpectedly saw movement. So did Mistix and he quickly increased the light emanating from his ring.

There were shiny creatures scuttling along the floor, crab-like and moving fast towards them. They were the same creatures Ethan had seen on the mantel. Ethan looked back the way they had come, only to see more of them coming around the corner, covering the floor and running up the walls. He didn't know what they were or what kind of threat they posed, but just the look of them made him shudder.

Mistix's hand gripped his arm.

'Run!'

They took off, tearing down the corridor, completely without stealth or care. The corridor turned left, so they skidded slightly as their momentum forced them sideways, before continuing with breathless desperation. This corridor was very long, possibly reaching half the length of the house. They passed doorway after doorway, all closed, with no obvious sign of an escape. The end of their route was getting closer, and the closer it got the more it became obvious that this was a dead end.

'There's nowhere to go!' Ethan puffed frantically. 'We'll have to try the doors!'

'Don't touch them!' Mistix barked, pulling himself up as the corridor finished. He spun around and began fiddling with his rings, manipulating several but with less certainty than his usual confidence.

Ethan watched as the creatures got closer. They were swarming everywhere including the ceiling, hundreds of red eyes honing in on their targets.

Mistix stood still and opened his arms as though to embrace the oncoming onslaught. Ethan nervously waited, anticipating some form of defence. But Mistix just stood there.

'What are you doing?' Ethan asked between gasps.

Mistix did not reply, and still the creatures came closer. The sound of their scuttling had become deafening on the bare surfaces, their echoes resonating around them. Ethan still searched for some kind of exit, but soon was transfixed by the metallic clattering wave coming towards them. Fifteen metres. Ten metres. Five metres. Ethan braced for a horrible death, picked apart by vicious robots.

'Two… one…' Mistix counted down. Just as the first robot was about to reach him, the sound of a thunder clap boomed out.

Ethan could literally see a physical distortion of air between Mistix's hands. The distortion flowed outwards, encompassing the horrors in front of them.

Like skin peeling off flesh, the creatures were torn off the walls, hurtling backwards down the corridor, flying through the air at an unbelievable speed. Several doors were blown inwards, and Ethan could feel a massive suction of air pulling him forwards. A loud shattering sound pierced through the thunder as the window at the far end of the corridor split apart, causing a tidal wave of creatures to flow out of the house. Within seconds the corridor had been cleared and Mistix allowed his hands to close.

'A magnetically charged sonic blast. Good thing those critters are made of metal.'

Ethan gasped. 'Are you serious? How much power do those rings have?'

'Considerable. If only they didn't take so long to recharge.'

'Somebody is bound to have heard all that noise.'

'Maybe. We need to be quick.' Mistix had already walked forward, pausing at a doorway which was now open. 'Now that's interesting. This could be something.'

Ethan caught up. 'It's just a white room.'

Mistix groaned. 'You don't know anything!' They went inside. It was a square white room, although Ethan could see flecks of silver imbedded into the wall itself. It looked like circuitry.

'It's a footprint room. Rooms like these are used to record important events. Meetings, strategic discussions, law making. It's no surprise the Deliverance has one. What happens in here is permanently encoded into the walls, a block-chain of information.' He fiddled with an emerald green ring, holding it high. 'Which can be intercepted.'

The ring released a pale-yellow light, and the room quickly responded. The walls lit up, a blazing white light enveloping them completely. Ethan no longer felt like he was in a room. The only word he could think of to describe what he felt was 'Heaven.' He felt like he was in Heaven.

Images began flickering around them like a movie in fast motion. People and furniture came and went in fractions of seconds. Faces and shapes blurred past them, rushing into nothingness only to be replaced by more movements, more footprints of the past. Suddenly they slowed, and a ghostly image of six people sitting around a table materialised beside them. Ethan jumped, as they all wore the ghastly masks he had seen earlier hanging from the walls, their tangible evil glaring outwards. Their bodies were covered in loose, black robes, and a deep, rich voice spoke like velvet.

'The Symbiosis exists, and I want it found!' The figure at the head of the table with glaring black eyes appeared to be the one speaking. 'Its location must be shielded, or we would have discovered it before now. The birds are *not* totally independent! They get their orders from somewhere and it's *not* from the Society. Our inside people have confirmed that. This stinking societal control is *not* going to continue, we are going to crush it or die trying, and I want every single Society member to witness their precious regime crumble.'

The figure to his left spoke. 'What's the status of our people in the Society?'

'They are integrated,' black eyes replied. 'And ready when we need them. Even now they are infiltrating their potions and weaponry. The Society has concentrated so much on external forces they haven't realised they are being invaded from within. And when we activate…' Black eyes clenched his fists together. 'I want to see that Ledren dead!' He groaned. 'But we have work to do until then. Continue recruitment. Reach out to our brothers and sisters so we can grow. I want half the population to call us… family.' He let out a deep, guttural laugh.

The table and figures blurred as images shifted. Eight masked figures materialised, sitting around a larger table, assuming their importance. Black eyes was speaking again, his body taut, his gravelly voice on fire.

'All these years the A.B.I. has been hidden away, the means to our deliverance and nobody knew about it! None of you! Our people have assimilated into every corner of this world and it's taken this long! I should burn the flesh off every one of you! How many years have we wasted?'

His left hand shot out, reaching towards the member at the opposite end of the table. His hand was gloved, a thick tensile material which glowed slightly as the electronics were activated. The member opposite shrieked and clutched his throat. Even though the gloved hand was some distance away, its invisible force was being felt.

'You were responsible for this!' He spoke low, threatening. 'It was your job to find the solution. And in the end…' His gritted teeth spat out the words, 'It wasn't even you that found the boy!'

Ethan was shocked. The means to their deliverance? Was black eyes talking about him? And what was the A.B.I.? Ethan had no time to contemplate this; black eyes was seeking revenge. A massive blast burst forth from his glove, tearing the member from his seating, turning him over backwards and hurling him against the wall behind, his robes flailing like laundry in the wind. The man crashed heavily to the floor, stationary.

Black eyes continued unabated.

'We are capturing the boy as I speak. Once he is here, we will make an assault on the Symbiosis and…'

Abruptly the image disappeared, and the room returned to being a room. Another image leapt forth from Mistix's rings and it hovered in front of them; the map of the house. But this time there were a number of red figures. Ethan counted three; then four; then five. Their animalistic representations were serpentine and foul, creatures from a nightmare.

'There are people in the house!' Mistix spat, annoyed.

Ethan's eyes opened wide. 'The Deliverance!'

'Presumably,' Mistix replied calmly, and looked around him. 'We need to go.'

He walked over to a far door, opposite to the one they had entered through, and set about opening it. A sudden clattering noise made Ethan whirl around. Rushing to the other door, his fears were confirmed. The creatures were back, pouring through the damaged window and heading straight for him.

'They're back! The crab things are coming!'

'Great,' Mistix muttered. The doorframe exploded, and the panel slid upwards. 'Get over here!' he barked. Ethan was already on his way and hurled himself through the opening. The creatures appeared, feverishly clambering towards them. Mistix directed his ring upwards and an even greater explosion singed the tops of their heads. The panel crashed down, bouncing once before settling and separating them from their attackers.

'Go! Go!'Mistix yelled. He had the lead, the map of the house hovering in front of them. The red figures were moving… fast. Two had split off from the main group, which now numbered six.

'They're on the level below us. They know we're here,' Mistix breathed. 'They're moving in to try and cut us off.'

They turned a corner; another corridor. A stairway lay to their left and down below they could hear the faint sound of feet running on wood. They kept running forwards. Another single figure had appeared on the map, not moving. This one had a beastly head with clawed hands.

'There's someone stationed at the window we

came through,' Ethan puffed, recognising the layout. His eyes focused alternatively between the map and reality, trying not to crash into something real.

Mistix's mind must have been racing, trying to work out the best route to evade their pursuers. Three more figures appeared, apparently two levels above them.

'Where did they come from?' Ethan huffed, turning a hard right past a room housing a collection of objects. In the fleeting second that he saw them, he noticed manacles on the walls and sharpened tools. *Items of torture?* Ethan wondered.

Mistix had his own train of thought.

'If we can make it to this next junction, I may be able to lead them down this other corridor and then jump up to the next level.'

'We want to get out though!' Ethan gasped. 'We need to go down!'

'Down is blocked,' Mistix retorted, and sure enough three more frightening figures had appeared. 'They've come through the main entrance, there's too many of them down there!'

'What about these others?' Ethan panted. 'They're upstairs!'

'Exactly!' Mistix replied. 'And that's where we're going. We just need them to think we are on a trajectory one way and then double back to get back to where they came from, before they do.'

Ethan understood. 'Because there is a way out there! They got in somehow, so we must be able to get out!'

'Brilliant,' Mistix said sarcastically. Ethan then

had a thought. What if they had used a ring like Mistix's and just materialised? He shuddered. There was no point in mentioning it, they had no choice.

Ahead was an open glass door. Bright light reached out to them from beyond and their eyes had to adjust as they crossed the threshold. They were now passing through a conservatory. Artificial light bathed down from above and they were surrounded by ferns, herbs and an assortment of smaller plants, some bearing fruits of various colours, others displaying berries that could have been tempting to try. It seemed somehow wrong to go tearing through such a place of tranquillity, but then again Ethan also felt like he wanted to run over the plants, knowing they belonged to the Deliverance. He wondered why they were here, but then it quickly occurred to him that the Deliverance were probably using them to produce their own potions; nothing like being self-sufficient.

They were running along a pathway between the plots of greenery. Some way in front was another glass door, this time closed. Mistix was obviously in no mood to see if it was locked. Holding up his fist, a burst of energy shot forth which found its target with ear shattering results. The glass ahead exploded, fragments blasted into little pieces, the shattering noise announcing their position in case there was any doubt. By the time they reached the spot, not only had the door been destroyed but half the wall around it.

Crunching on glass, they tore through the devastation to another corridor beyond which led them to a crossway. There were corridors to the left and right, and further up ahead was another stairway. It was here that Mistix stopped. The map hovered in front of them, and they watched their pursuers above and below. Beneath them they were coming from two different directions, obviously aiming to come in behind them but also upwards from the stairway ahead. The group above them also appeared to be heading towards the same stairway. In fact, they were getting very close, running in the corridor directly on top of their heads. Each second was getting them closer and closer. Yet Mistix still hesitated.

'Let's go!' Ethan urged, tugging his arm. Mistix pulled away. 'Not yet,' he responded, watching the map intently.

The figures above were closest. They passed above the two blue figures representing Ethan and Mistix. Mistix waited a couple seconds more, and then spat out his order.

'Now!'

He led the way to the left, and then turned again left at the next junction, now going in the same direction they had come but down the outside of the conservatory. They were back tracking and were now closer to their destination than their pursuers.

Ethan felt the adrenaline pounding. Mistix was fast and he knew that he was slowing so that Ethan could keep up. It wasn't long before they reached a staircase, and both bounded up it, first one floor, and then the next. They had increased the lead on their pursuers; their change in direction had proved useful, but Ethan's legs had started to feel like jelly. He definitely wasn't used to this type of vigorous exercise.

The room they sought was now ahead. Ethan tried to imagine the form of their escape. A lift? A walkway? He'd take anything to get out of this crazy house.

They burst through the doorway, senses alert for any danger. Like Mistix, he took in their surroundings in an instant.

The room itself was not large. Four strange structures stood in front of them. Cocoon-shaped and made of metal, they curved around in a criss-crossed pattern which reminded Ethan of the transportation ring with its metallic growing arms as it swallowed him. His heart sank as he realised that this was probably exactly what it was, and the means to get out of the house. There seemed nothing of any importance otherwise: a fireplace, a cupboard, strange, unidentifiable decorations on the wall and a single chair in one corner, facing the cocoons.

Mistix wasted no time. He was already opening one of the cocoons and studying the interior.

'Get in,' he demanded. 'It's a transportation pod. I'll activate it and follow in another one.'

Disbelieving that he had to go through the transportation process once more, Ethan took a deep breath and squeezed past Mistix, jamming himself into the back of the pod. He was already feeling claustrophobic, peering through the gaps in the metal like he would out of a jail cell. Mistix slammed the door shut and without hesitation brought his hand down hard on a big green button at the front of the pod. Ethan instantly felt a strange charge of electricity pass through him as it hummed into life, and an urgent thought broke free from his lips.

'But where am I going?'

There was no answer, and his trepidation was only enhanced as an explosion next to him made him jump and he hit his head on the top of the cocoon. A second explosion made him completely lose balance as he tried to retreat from its source. Two of the pods were now on fire. Mistix was blowing them up.

What happened next was over in a second. The first of their pursuers tore into the room, his fitted black mask glaring at them with hate and determination. His fist was raised and aimed directly at Mistix, who instinctively spun around after completing his destruction of the two pods and in one lithe movement, flung himself through the air, turning his own fist towards the newcomer. Simultaneously there were two flashes; two forces in direct opposition to each other, reaching out to strike their opponent down. The whole room lit up, before a third flash blinded Ethan completely as he and his cocoon blinked out of existence.

CHAPTER 16

Jessica was working. Hidden away in a room behind the one the teenagers had entered into earlier, this was her real office. The dowdy desk and shelves of awards were just an unassuming cover. No need to advertise the technology she uses, in this, her true working space. The wall in front held a patchwork of electronic data. She had been searching relentlessly for information about Ethan and his past. But true to her profession, she knew that being a thorough detective meant that she could not just confine her investigations to the main subject, as every person who touched another may leave a ripple of information. You could learn a lot about a person, by investigating the people that knew them. In Ethan's case, he knew so few people; she did not have a wide field to cover. But the information that was scrolling in front of her, made her feel very worried.

'Oh dear,' she uttered, her uneasiness palpable. 'I knew as soon as I saw them something wasn't right. That boy needs to be warned.' She looked down at her wrist-o-gram, which remained silent despite her attempts to bring it to life. 'Why hasn't he got it on? Something must have happened.' She looked back to the data in front. 'It was so obvious I should have said something else at the time. And they know I know. I'm sure of it. I just didn't expect this.'

Some more information flashed up. 'But I'm not beaten. They don't call me detective of the year for nothing. Sometimes it comes down to knowing someone who knows someone. Or in this case, knows them.'

Plumping up her purple permed hair, Jessica set to work.

It was easier this time. There was less disorientation, less confusion, less suffocation; perhaps because he was getting used to it, or perhaps because the pod was a real machine rather than a condensed miniature version as a ring. Either way, as soon as he reappeared, Ethan pushed the door open and stumbled out, glad to be released. Gratefully, he was also alone. He was in a darkened cavern, possibly underground, and feeling completely lost and out of place. It had occurred to him that the pod may have taken him to its last destination, in which case there might be others from the Deliverance lurking around. Or Mistix may have sent him somewhere completely different. He cursed that Mistix hadn't told him, but this time he had to pull back from his annoyance. There was no doubt Mistix had just saved his life, and at what cost to his?

He turned back to the pod to scour the area next to it for Mistix's arrival. He waited anxiously, his eyes darting back over his shoulder and to the sides, expecting somebody to appear at any second. As the minutes passed, it became obvious that Mistix was not following, and the blood slowly drained from Ethan's face as he realised he may not have gotten out alive.

He swore savagely and would have punched something if he wasn't surrounded by rock. What the hell was he supposed to do now? He was now alone and basically defenceless, bar the unknown vial he still carried in his pocket. And despite his dislike for Mistix, he hadn't wanted him to be harmed, especially in his role as some kind of personal bodyguard. Which, Ethan had to remind himself, he had never asked for in the first place.

His thoughts turned back to the Footprint room, and the revelation that he was somehow the missing link for the Deliverance. What was that about? Did they really think he was so important? The only thing special about him was the space chip inside his head, and if they wanted that they could have it!

There was, of course, the fact that he couldn't remember a damn thing. Did somebody deliberately wipe his mind, and if so, how and for what purpose? Perhaps he knew something that the Deliverance wanted, but then who would have wiped his mind? The Society? Maybe *they* knew him, before he was a patient in the hospital. A sudden thought struck. Could he have been working for *them*? They employed somebody as young as Mistix, so why not himself?

Apart from the fact that he had no useful skills, of course, or at least none that he knew of. He had so many questions and no answers to any of it. None! And that's even before he questioned the intention of the girls. Who was good and who was bad? What were their objectives towards him? Should he be concerned about them as Mistix suggested, or better yet, how concerned should he have been about Mistix following him whether he wanted him there or not? This question posed Ethan difficulties considering

Mistix may just have sacrificed his life for him, so this was, yet again, another point of confusion.

Running his hands through his tousled hair, he took a deep breath and considered his next move. He couldn't just hang around here. Two of the pods were destroyed but what of the third? If Mistix hadn't destroyed it or got into it to escape, then presumably the Deliverance could follow him. The interesting question was, did they know who he was, or did they just think he was some random intruder? If they knew who he was, without a doubt they would continue to chase him. This thought alone spurred Ethan on to start moving.

His options seemed limited. Although he was standing in an open cavern, there only seemed to be one way forward: a pathway snaking off to the right. Treading softly, he set off, trying not to dislodge any noisy pebbles or rocks underfoot.

The path wound upwards, slightly twisting in its route until it levelled out. It was lighter up ahead and instinctively he tried to keep in the shadows closer to the wall. Slowing, he peered cautiously around a curve and instantly froze. It was another cavern, smaller than the last, but there were Nuns. Lots of them. Standing silent and stationary together like a crowd at a party in a waxwork's museum. There must have been at least fifty of them, their soulless faces all pointing in the same direction, blankly staring sightlessly ahead.

Ethan had to consciously stop himself from retreating at the spectacle of the black and white ensemble. But it became quickly apparent that they were not moving. He watched for some minutes but there was no sign of life. He wondered if they were switched off or shut down, perhaps to conserve energy, or maybe they had nothing to do. Or perhaps they were waiting for something.

Ethan pursed his lips. He had to get past them; there was no escape from the direction he had come from.

He looked down at his feet and picked up a small rock. Unsure if this was a good idea or not, he tested the weight in his hand for a few seconds and then hurled it across the breadth of the area. Landing close to the Nuns on the far side, it clipped another rock before thudding into the earth. Ethan waited, but there was no response or reaction from the Nuns. They appeared to be completely dormant.

Gritting his teeth, he tentatively took a few steps forward. He was now in plain sight of the robots, if they cared to notice, which apparently, they did not. There was still no response.

With some determination, he moved forward, one step at a time, silently moving one foot faster than the last. His eyes were glued to the Nuns, searching for any flicker of movement. Up close, they somehow seemed even more unnerving than when he had met them previously, as before they had life, but this bunch were like the standing dead. It didn't take much imagination to foresee them coming to life with outstretched hands, reaching and clawing for him, or chasing him with their angry red eyes.

Fighting back his inner thoughts, he made the last few steps to reach the other side and hurried along the pathway which continued upwards. He finally felt like he could breathe again.

The chamber remained motionless for only a few seconds more, before fifty heads all turned in unison to stare at his retreating figure.

Jingles was laughing. Her dark curls bobbed up and down, uncontrollable like the frenzied noise erupting from her lips.

'You should have seen it, Syntax. It was fantastic! They swallowed them up like it was Christmas lunch. And then the birds came and blew them all up. I can't *wait* until we fully activate.'

Syntax looked dirty. 'That was not planned! Control your urges and keep to what was agreed!'

Jingles sidled up to him. 'I've got it all recorded,' she said smoothly. 'You'll be able to watch it.' Her voice was teasing. 'And not only that...' she continued, 'But *guess* who I saw?' With a rapid flick of a ring on her finger, Ethan's image rose up in front of them. '*He* was there,' she spat, 'walking around like a fool!'

Syntax looked interested. 'Where did he go?'

Jingles snorted. 'He was sucked away by a transportation ring. A Leech was about to get him too!'

Syntax swung around, his hand shooting out to find solace around Jingles' neck. His eyes were full of rage and Jingles choked as he tightened his grip.

'You imbecile! You could've ruined everything!'

Despite her lack of air, Jingles still managed a smirk. She grabbed Syntax's hand with both of hers and yanked it away.

'It would have spat him out!' she retorted angrily. 'He's not to its taste!'

'We don't know that for sure!' Syntax hissed. 'The chip's effect could be variable!'

'Whatever!' Jingles replied, disinterested, and reached behind her. In her hands, she now held the sphere Syntax had shown his brother and Ethan earlier. A new glint appeared in her eyes, which somehow transferred itself to Syntax.

'Are we doing it?' she asked, breathless with anticipation.

Syntax's anger suddenly subsided, and he stared at his companion. A single thought passed through them, joined by their common goal.

Slowly, he smiled, and Jingles upper lip curled at the corner in reply.

Ethan continued to walk upwards. He'd come to a fork in the tunnel and chose the route that appeared to lead still higher. He rationalised that he'd be able to get a better idea of where he was if he ever came to an exit by going upwards. Going sideways could just lead him deeper into rock.

It occurred to him that perhaps below was being used as a storage area for the Nuns; somewhere to keep them when they weren't needed. Which meant he could well be in another lair of the Deliverance. He was pretty sure the Nuns were their pawns.

Eventually the path levelled out to another open area and he paused. He looked down at his wrist and thought how now would be a good time to talk to Jessica. He was actually surprised she hadn't contacted him earlier as he got the feeling things moved fast with her and she may have more information to share.

It then struck him that something else was strange. The blue light wasn't on, which meant the wrist-o-gram was turned off. He touched the side of the device and the light lit up. Almost immediately Jessica's face appeared, hovering in front of him.

'Ethan!' she exclaimed, her eyes portraying concern and relief at the same time. 'I've been trying to contact you. Are you okay, dear?'

Ethan spoke softly in reply, unsure if he may be heard by somebody.

'Yes, I'm fine. I didn't know the wrist-o-gram was off.' He frowned. 'I don't know why it wasn't on,' he added.

Jessica spoke the obvious answer. 'Somebody must have turned it off, dear.' She paused to let this sink in, before breaking the silence. 'Where are your friends?'

Ethan shrugged. 'I don't know; we all got separated.' He briefly explained how. Jessica suddenly looked very grave.

'That may be for the best.'

Ethan was surprised by her statement. 'Why?'

Jessica sighed. 'I've been doing some investigating Ethan, and I've come across some interesting facts.' She took a breath and continued.

'A number of years ago, there was a family of four sisters, two pairs of twins. They were all highly intelligent – geniuses in fact – and had a strong interest in the development of potions and technological gadgets. It was an interest they had inherited from the rest of their family, including their parents and uncle.'

Ethan's face had become impassive, realising where this was leading.

'As a family they had made some remarkable advances in the field, even though at times their motivations for doing so differed. The twins' different persuasions made co-operation strained, at best. When the sisters were still quite young, they were working on an experiment which resulted in a big fight. There was a fire and explosion, and two of the sisters and their mother were killed. There were rumours that the other two sisters had been responsible, although nothing was ever proven.'

Ethan shook his head, stunned. 'You're talking about Rose and Violet.'

Jessica nodded. 'Ethan, do you remember when you were at my place, when I mentioned about their shoes?'

Ethan nodded. 'Why did you say that?'

'I realised at once when I saw them. The two girls are exactly the same height, but their shoes were *different heights*. They wear very thick make up and have their hair styled exactly the same. As they are noticeably different weights it has been easy to convince people that they are identical twins. *But they are not. They are only sisters.*'

Ethan went pale, the ramifications of this sinking in and the realisation of the truth.

'So that means…'

Jessica finished his sentence in a whisper. 'They

may both be evil!'

Ethan shook his head, disbelieving. 'They can't be…'

'Somebody turned off the wrist-o-gram, so I couldn't contact you, Ethan. Who would have had the opportunity?'

Ethan remembered the time Rose had held his hand. And he had only been close to the group he had been travelling with.

'Any of them could have done it…' His voice trailed off.

Jessica's voice became clipped. 'Keep your mind open, Ethan. Now stay where you are, I'm tracking you and will get you some help.'

'Well, where am I?'

Jessica paused. 'You seem to be in a passageway in the mountain behind the convent of the Sisters of the Living Dead. You won't be able to get out easily. Find somewhere you can hide, and I'll be in touch.'

Her face disappeared.

Ethan stood dazed. He had not expected Jessica's revelation about the girls and it changed everything. Their pretence at being twins, their insistence that people could choose who they want to be, the impression that maybe they cared about him; it was all a lie.

He cursed and turned around, only to have his heart leap into his throat in sudden and unexpected shock.

Standing in front of him were Rose and Violet.

CHAPTER 17

The girls didn't look happy. Even Rose had an expression on her face which he had not seen before. Was it anger, or something else?

Violet spoke. 'Why was Jessica investigating *us*?'

Did she sound threatening, or was it just his imagination? Instinctively, Ethan fumbled for a vial in his pocket.

'I don't know,' he replied warily. 'I didn't know she was going to do that. It was the first contact I've had with her since before we went to Mildred's.'

He twisted his neck and tried to scratch. The collar around it was suddenly uncomfortable.

'That was not her business,' Rose said softly, and tugged at her own collar with irritation. 'Our family has got nothing to do with her.' The girls had obviously heard the entire conversation with Jessica.

Ethan stepped forward. 'Is it true?' he blurted out, longing to know, though unsure of his wisdom in asking. 'What happened to your sisters?' he demanded, tugging once more at his collar. Surely it was getting hot. Both girls were also pulling at theirs, apparently as uncomfortable as he was.

'What's going on?' Violet exclaimed, forgetting her conversation with Ethan and now trying to pull the collar away from her skin with both hands.

'It's hurting,' Rose exclaimed, panic rising in her voice.

The three of them stood clutching at their throats, grappling uselessly with their devices as they remained firmly enclosed around their necks. That was, until the collar around Rose gave a small explosion. She shrieked as smoke blew into her face. Panicked, she grasped the damaged collar and ripped it free, sending it flying through the air, just missing Ethan as it sailed past. Violet's and Ethan's collars also shot out sparks and blew up, causing both to cry out in alarm, but the damage enabled them to tear it from their scorched throats. They were finally liberated. It took them a few seconds to fully digest what had just happened. Rose and Violet stared at each other, disbelieving. After a lifetime of imprisonment, they could at last breathe and move without influence, without constriction.

And yet, a sense of anxiety was already mounting, as both had reached behind to cover the mark at the base of their necks.

In the streets of the city, panic and surprise had gripped its residents. The roads were littered with fallen collars. People rushed around using anything to conceal the emblems at the base of their necks; scarves, coat collars, the palms of their hands. Emotions were conflicted. There was a sense of relief at being free from the unnatural attachment that had been part of them since they were five years old. But the overwhelming feeling was of fear. Who had done this? Why did it happen? What consequences would it bring? Yet there was more to it than that. Their very soul was being exposed to the world. And people were already taking advantage. An old man cowered in a corner as three other younger men leered over him. The upside-down hearts on their necks lined up one after the other, the first time to see daylight since they were children.

'They got it wrong!' the old man stammered, holding his hands up for protection. 'The heart should be the other way around. I'm one of you!'

His protestations were ignored as the men moved in to attack. The old man screamed out to the birds. By the time the first one arrived, the three men were scuttling into a nearby building, and the old man lay face down on the ground, the bone white upright heart on his neck slowly being covered by dark blood oozing from a deep wound in his scalp.

Rose spoke to Violet. 'What's happened?' she exclaimed, transfixed on her sister. The two stared at each other. 'Do you think...?' She didn't finish her sentence.

Violet just nodded and simply said, 'Yes.' There seemed to be an understanding between the two, which was not lost on Ethan. He was feeling more and more like these girls knew a lot more than they had revealed to him. And it was time he found out what it was. He pulled his hand out of his pocket, clenching the vial inside with sweaty hands.

'Tell me what's going on,' he demanded, fraught with exasperation, suspicion and tiredness. 'You know something! Why are you here? This is where the Nuns live!'

Violet looked dark. 'Jessica shouldn't have told you about us. But trust us, Ethan. We are here to help you.'

The girls could see his determination, and he kept

walking forward towards them, his breath catching in his throat.

'I need to know,' he said softly but decisively, and appeared to be trying to get in behind them by circling them. 'If you have nothing to hide, show me your necks.'

Immediately the girls bristled, moving cautiously so that they were facing him at all times.

'No, Ethan!' Rose responded. 'It's private. It's not for other people to see.'

He noticed Violet had reached into her potion bag, her hand lingering inside. Would she attack him? If she was evil, then he couldn't doubt it.

'Keep back, Ethan,' Violet warned.

'You know us!' Rose affirmed. 'We are on the same side!'

'Then show me your neck!' Ethan responded, circling more rapidly as though he had some chance of getting behind them. The three were turning in unison as though on some giant turn table. The more Ethan thought about the girls, the more convinced he was about their lies. The two of them were hiding their true identities by dressing alike, treating other people like fools. Violet had callously turned the girl selling the statues into an old hag; she had told him the potion would wear off, but that was only her word. And what were they doing here? How could they have got here without the Nuns knowing? They must be working with them. He remembered Violet's impotence at protecting them from the Nuns when they had attacked; her firepower was not able to damage a single one of them. Was that because she hadn't wanted to?

'Do you work for the Deliverance?' Ethan barked. He turned the vial in his palm, questioning himself whether he would need to use it.

'Of course not,' Violet responded calmly, withdrawing her hand slowly from her bag. Ethan could see a glint of glass. He stepped forward, now completely facing Rose, a metre apart, and looked deep into her eyes. 'Show me your neck.' This time, it was not a demand. He was begging her.

'No,' she gasped, shaking her head. Ethan's hand holding the potion lifted slightly, but this was all that Violet needed to react. She lunged forward in an attempt to grasp his wrist. Ethan saw her movement and pulled his arm backwards, but too late to avoid her motion. The end result caused Violet to knock his forearm hard, forcing it backwards, the momentum tearing the vial from his grasp. It flew up into the air, the black liquid spinning inside, slicing its path towards the ground.

They all turned, suddenly spellbound on its trajectory. The vial smashed, several metres to the right of Rose, and immediately blue smoke began rising from the splattered pool. Strangely Ethan recognised it.

'It's Father's new potion!' Rose screamed. 'Run!'

Ethan understood. It was the potion Camdex had used to make the hole in the table. But in that demonstration, he had used only a few drops. And they had just broken the whole bottle!

The three separated. Ethan sprinted back towards the passage he had come from. As he ran, he turned and was shocked to see the centre of the room had disappeared into nothingness. Like a ripple on a lake, the nothingness spread, the ground dissolving as though it were made of nothing more than sugar. He made it to the edge of the room before hearing the girls scream. Caught up in the wake of the potion, the ground beneath them evaporated, just before they reached the extent of its field. Violet's robotic arm frantically clawed for a hold on the rock face as she fell, digging in for her life. Rose fell further, reaching for the only the thing within her grasp; Violet's legs. The two hung precariously, supported only by the strength of Camdex's technology. Their terrified screams reverberated in the enclosed cavern. They were calling for help and they were calling Ethan's name.

Ethan stopped, aghast at their situation. He took a step towards the girls but then hesitated, assessing the situation. The ground seemed to have stabilised. The hole wasn't spreading any further but had consumed almost the entire cavern floor. A narrow strip of earth and rock remained around the perimeter, barely enough room to support one person. It could, however, potentially enable him to move to the point above the girls, which was almost on the opposite side to where he was. There was no question. He had to try to help them.

What he was going to do if he reached them, he wasn't sure.

Pressing himself against the wall, he tentatively tested the ground next to him. It felt stable, but his gaze kept diverting to the chasm at his feet. Looking down, it plunged into darkness below. It would not be a survivable fall.

Sidestepping, he took the first few steps, holding his breath as though it were his last. The ground held his weight, and he kept going. He could see Rose trying to find some grip with her feet on the rock face, which was only serving to precariously cause them both to swing. Violet's human hand was also scrabbling for traction, unfortunately raining chunks of earth down on Rose. Ethan furtively glanced from his feet to the girls and back again, acutely aware of the race against time. But then he became aware of something else. Above the centre of the great chasm, a swirling gaseous cloud was forming. It started off as faint wispy tendrils, but then grew like an approaching thunderstorm. And Ethan remembered. In the laboratory a cloud had formed above the hole in the table before it reassembled itself. But this time Rose and Violet were clinging on in the middle of it. If the ground reformed around them, they would be as good as dead.

Now feeling panicked, Ethan hurried. He scuttled sideways around the narrow ledge like one of the metal crabs he'd escaped from earlier. As he moved, parts of the ledge crumbled at the edges, ensuring his momentum onwards. The girls were screaming out his name to help, the terror in their voices saturating his ears and helping to form the sweat which was now dripping down his face.

In astonishingly short time, he reached the area above the girls. Their distraught faces looked up; splattered with dirt and imploring his assistance, the fear in their eyes was burning into his soul. Hurriedly

Ethan kneeled, noting that there was slightly more room on this area of the ledge to allow him to do so. A faint wind rustled his hair and cooled his face, reminding him of the ever-increasing swirl of the dark cloud in front of him.

Violet's hand was deeply embedded in rock but it was crumbling as he watched. It would not hold much longer. As though in slow motion, he saw Rose's grip slip and she slid further down Violet's legs.

'Ethan!' she screeched, a sudden look of realisation dawning, and their eyes met. 'I can't hold on!' she panted. She was breathless with terror. They both seemed to freeze, staring at each other, their silence communicating the inevitable. Ethan's heart sank in fear and his burnt throat turned cold. He could see her hands losing strength.

Forcing concentration, Ethan reached down his hand towards the girls, straining to make the distance without toppling over the ledge himself. His arm was too short. Violet was reaching upwards with her free hand, but they could not connect. He looked again at Violet's wide-open eyes as she strained to reach him, and then down to Rose, whose eyes had suddenly developed tears. Once again, their gaze lingered. This time he saw her face change from desperation to surrender.

'Ethan!' she rasped, swallowing hard. She opened her mouth, sucking in air as though ready to release a long-held pressure inside of her. With the loudest voice she could muster, she cried out, her heart exploding outwards so the whole world could hear.

'I'm not bad! I'm *good*...!'

Her grip failed, and she slid off Violet's legs, her impassive and tearful face staring upwards as she was lost in blackness.

Ethan and Violet simultaneously screamed out her name, their hearts following hers into oblivion. Without Rose's weight on her legs, Violet was able to reach Ethan's hand, but the two were too weak in their grief to move further. They hung precariously immobile.

It was then that it happened. Instant and complete confusion gripped Ethan as he was taken by surprise. A searing pain enveloped his head. A pain so strong that his screams drowned out even that of Violet's unrelenting anguish beneath him, encompassing every sinew and fibre of his body. Through tormented eyes, his world turned blue as he was swallowed by a disorientating haze. His brain was on fire. With his free hand he clutched his head in agony, no longer able to focus on his rescue or contemplate rational thought, completely detached from what was happening around him. With one final shriek, he passed out, and toppled helplessly over the edge. Violet was knocked from her position and the two of them tumbled after Rose.

A howling wind tore around the cavern and the ground reformed, solid as though it always had been.

CHAPTER 18

Jingles stood with her arms crossed, a sneer of delight plastered across her youthful face. Syntax stood next to his monolithic black column, apparently not as impressed but satisfied nonetheless. They had succeeded; their plan was almost complete.

In front of them was Ethan. They had activated the space chip and he had come. Unwillingly, of course, but here he was, strung up like a piece of meat caught in a web. His arms and legs were splayed, pulled out to the sides by snake-like attachments which wound their way behind and upwards, connected to a huge star-shaped computer immediately above. A circlet had been placed around his forehead, metallic connections digging deep into his temples and small pincers pulling his eyelids back, so they could not close. His head was bowed, but slowly his consciousness was returning, and the fear began spreading across his face as he stared ahead. Opposite him, as a holographic image, was an old man, strung up in what looked to be a similar contraption to the one that he himself was imprisoned in. Except this man's face was impassive and pale with eyes that were soul-less and black like pools of oil, and from his gaping mouth there hung a tube, forced down his throat to reach far down inside him. He was clothed in nothing more than rags. The scene was grotesque and terrifying.

Ethan struggled frantically, trying to twist his body out of his bindings, but they were immovable.

He screamed for help before his watering eyes settled in on the other two figures in front of him. He recognised Syntax immediately, although barely registered the girl beside him. Glancing sideways, there were also numerous Nuns, standing around the perimeter of the room, motionless and watching.

And then he saw Violet. She was flanked by three Nuns, but they were holding her arms firmly, obviously a prisoner. He was relieved at seeing her safe and well, but she was clearly not okay. Her face was stained with tears.

'Violet!' Ethan croaked, his throat dry. 'Rose...?'

Violet shook her head, distressed. 'I got caught up in the field of the space chip and got transported here with you. I don't know what's happened to her!'

She turned to her uncle. 'I have to go find her!' she demanded, almost hysterical.

Syntax snapped. 'You're staying here.'

As if in response, the Nuns seemed to grip her tighter, sinking their pale fingers deeper into her flesh. Violet struggled.

'Let me go!'

Ethan could see her trying to raise her mechanical arm, but the Nuns' strength seemed to be a match for hers.

'Uncle, please!'

Uncle and niece held their gaze on each other, and Ethan could see the resemblance between them. Not only because they had the same pale blue eyes, but both were resolute and committed to their actions.

'No,' Syntax said, unyielding. He turned back to

the monolith. The decision was made.

Jingles stepped forward. 'He's busy. If you distract him…' She smiled. 'I'll get the Nuns to chop your arm off; your good one!'

One Nun opened her mouth, volunteering. 'I'll do it.'

Jingles acknowledged her. 'Thank you. I'll let you know.'

Violet clamped her mouth shut, seething and distraught. Ethan noted that she didn't have her bag of potions with her. She probably lost it during the fall.

He looked to Syntax. 'What do you want?' he gasped, breathing fast and irregularly as panic gripped his heart. 'Let me go!' He struggled once more. Syntax ignored him completely, as though he had not even spoken. He was doing something to the monolith.

Jingles stepped forward, eager to talk to him.

'We have only just activated the space chip to get you here, Ethan.' She smiled innocently. 'And I can't tell you how much work it took to get that decrepit technology working again, even though in the end we only transported you about a hundred metres! So, you're not going anywhere, honey.'

Ethan gulped in some air, trying to steady himself. 'You put the space chip in me?' he spat angrily.

Jingles laughed and shook her curls. 'No, Ethan,' she said, as though talking to a child. 'You've had that inside you since you were five. Camdex didn't want to lose his A.B.I.; at all costs.'

Ethan was confused. 'What does that mean?'

'Alternate. Biological. Insertion.' Jingles spoke the words slowly. 'You want to know why you're so special? It's because you can replace *him*.' She indicated the decrepit old man opposite, and Ethan stared at him once more.

'What's he *for*?' he gasped.

'He's very *unique*.' She paused, building up the suspense, then speaking slowly and deliberately as though giving a lecture. 'He's fed through that tube in his gullet. All his bodily functions are maintained fully by the technology around him without any need for him to be disconnected from his purpose. It allows him to control the birds! And more,' she added mysteriously. 'And nobody knows it except us. Apart from Camdex, of course, who put him there.'

Ethan couldn't keep his eyes off the horrifying scene in front of him.

'Camdex did that?'

Jingles smiled. 'Not so *good* after all, is he?' she taunted, absently twirling her curls. 'You were both bred to be fodder for this machine, which is called the Symbiosis. This man controls the computer, and the computer controls this man! When Camdex built it all those years ago, he knew it could always be hacked. So, he needed to incorporate an element into it that was unique, that could not be compromised. It had to be biological, rather than technological. So, he decided it had to be a person, and that person had to be…' she paused before spitting out the word, 'Good.' Jingles sighed, somehow enjoying the explanation. 'Like yourself, this man was genetically engineered so that his DNA integrated perfectly with the system. Once he was old enough, his memory was wiped, and he became part of the Symbiosis, completely unaware of anything except that which the computer shows him. He sees everything the birds sees, everything the monitors see. He can control them.' Jingles' face contorted in a sudden flash of accomplishment, and she said smoothly, 'He would feel very powerful.'

Ethan couldn't help but feel that somehow, she was jealous. It was then that he realised that she was mad. And that made her especially dangerous. But his heart was sinking as her words were permeating his tired mind.

'What do you mean I'm genetically engineered?'

'You were cloned off him, so that you could take over when he dies.' She gave a shrill laugh.

Ethan's stomach sunk. This decrepit old man was his twin? And not even a real twin. A clone. He was now more alone than ever.

Jingles continued. 'The trouble was, *you* didn't turn out quite the way Camdex planned. Even though you were copied fifty years apart, it turns out that one is still created good...' She clasped her hands, enjoying the moment. 'And one was created evil.' Her delight was evident as her words sunk in.

'But I'm not evil,' Ethan said quietly.

Jingles held up her hand and an image of Ethan's face appeared from one of her rings. The image turned around to focus on the back of his neck. The heart emblazoned on his skin was clearly upside down.

'When Camdex realised you were evil he not only implanted the space chip so that he could always find you, but also an experimental inhibitor which would dampen down any evil thoughts. Essentially, he made you non-evil, a child walking around with an incomplete personality. But you were still too much of a risk for him. If you were ever integrated into the Symbiosis the birds would do *your* will, so he banished you from here and you grew up with a family not your own, thousands of kilometres away.'

'That's not true!' Ethan said, but his heart had also already latched onto the fact that she had said he had a *family*. And it lifted him ever so slightly.

'I can turn off your inhibitor from one of my rings,' Jingles teased. 'Do you want to see? How would your thoughts change?' She waved her hand tauntingly in front of him. 'When the Deliverance found you at last, they took you, wiped your memory immediately and then lost you again when they were attacked by the security forces. Fortunately, the Nuns scanned you in the hospital and found out you had the space chip implanted, and then *we* were clever enough to devise how to activate it.'

'You work for the Deliverance then,' Ethan concluded.

'No!' Jingles screamed, suddenly enraged. '*They* work for *us*! We started the Deliverance, and they answer to *us*!'

Syntax raised an eyebrow at her outburst, but this was not uncommon, and he was used to it. She was an eccentric genius and he tolerated her; for the moment, anyway. His concern was not what was happening between Ethan and Jingles anyway; he didn't care. All he cared about was the next step, which was about to begin.

With some finality, Syntax entered the last instruction into the monolith's electronics. It was done. Everything was complete. He spoke, his words causing a wave of fear to swell through Ethan's stomach. 'I'm ready. Do it. Do it now.' He looked meaningfully at Jingles.

Jingles held up her hand and smiled. 'I'm turning your inhibitor off. Goodbye *good* Ethan. Hello… *evil* Ethan.'

With a touch of her finger, she activated the circuitry on one of her rings.

Ethan's eyes flickered within their pincer constraints. A cloud passed over his mind, but then settled just as quickly and he felt his thoughts clearer than ever. Something was different. Violet watched him as he perused his surroundings, taking it all in as though seeing it for the first time. He looked at Violet, held captive by the Nuns, and then turned away, disinterested. Instead, he focused on Jingles.

'Turn it on,' he demanded. 'I want access.'

Jingles clasped her hands excitedly, and then held her left hand up towards Syntax. Syntax reciprocated, holding his right towards her. There was power being generated inside this room. Black light encompassed the pair before splitting off into two. One ray shot off to encompass the monolith behind them, while the second beam found its destination in Ethan. The monolith came to life, the empty blackness of its core becoming deeper and stirring, its depths swirling in mystery while radiating blackness outwards. For Ethan it was the opposite. It was like he became death itself. His eyes clouded over, no longer green and alive but blackened like the darkness in his evil heart. His body stiffened and then relaxed as it became redundant. It was his mind that was important now as he became integrated into the system, part of a living, complex machine that needed him to survive. The feeding tube extended from behind him, breaching between his teeth and forcing itself into his gullet, ready to supply sustenance for the remainder of his life.

On the hologram in front, the old man suddenly stirred as his role was fractured. By Ethan becoming one with the Symbiosis, Syntax had ensured that it caused negative feedback to the original system, extricating the man from the machine. He was released from his bindings and he crumpled to the floor.

Ethan's head lifted slightly as he began to receive data, his mind seeing more than his eyes could ever possibly do. The world around him was changing. No longer was he restricted to one narrow viewpoint in one direction. He could see everywhere, a collage of everything every bird or monitor in existence could show. And he could hear it all, each sound blending in perfectly with its surroundings, everything making complete and utter sense to him. People were moving and scurrying beneath him, beside him, around him, completely unaware of his presence, as he watched and evaluated, and judged. Jingles had said he would feel powerful. Well, this was better than that. He judged and saw *everything*, and he liked it.

But above all, as he watched the people, he could see the hearts on the back of their necks. Those that were right side up were like bait to him. He saw them, and he wanted to destroy.

The birds that he now controlled suddenly had new commands. As the instructions filtered through, something else was stirring on the streets below. Darkened shapes were appearing; shifting images slowly gaining substance, the signal from the monolith ensuring a wave of blackness was bringing to life everywhere the terrors from people's nightmares. If anyone ever had any doubt that Time Leeches were real, this doubt was now dispelled as the creatures began appearing in people's workplaces and in their homes. The screams formed a cacophony of noise, reverberating through Ethan's mind, filling him. And he wanted more. As people called for assistance from the birds, he allowed them to swoop down close before firing on the helpless humans below.

This was only the beginning of his reign, and the massacre had started.

CHAPTER 19

The holographic image of the old man had changed to show the carnage in the streets outside. Violet watched with horror as people were cut down by the birds or swallowed whole by the Leeches. She couldn't take her eyes off it, mesmerised until the image began to blur. But then she realised it wasn't the image that was blurring; it was the air in front. A darkened, evil image was appearing, and she recognised it as a Time Leech.

Violet recoiled and struggled violently against the Nuns. Jingles saw what was happening and couldn't contain her excitement.

'You had a Time Leech attached to you!' she squealed. 'Fantastic!'

'Do something or it'll get you as well!' Violet screamed.

'Ha!' Jingles replied. 'Actually, it won't! What people haven't realised, because they're too stupid, is that the Leeches only like *good* people. It is easier for them to form a connection, less resistance, which is why they are absolutely perfect for helping us to halve the population.'

Violet stood shocked, unaware that this had been the intention of the mad woman in front of her. And of her own uncle, who was a part of it.

'Uncle, please!' she implored, desperately trying to break free from the Nuns.

Syntax looked, assessing the situation, and Violet felt sick as she saw the indecision in his face. She did, of course, know that he was evil, but she thought their blood ties would be stronger. But here, as he stood thinking before her, it became very clear the extent of the chasm between them as the response to his choice was not readily answered.

'Uncle?' she said more softly, questioning.

Syntax stepped forward. 'The time for *good* is over. It's *our* turn.'

They stared at each other, and the Leech fully materialised. Violet held her breath.

Syntax looked at the Nuns. 'Let her go' And then to Violet. 'Get out of here.' It seemed being family did have some influence on her Uncle. At least he wasn't going to let her be killed by a Leech.

The nuns released their grip and Violet was free. The Leech had started moving towards her.

Violet chided herself at how stupid she had been in underestimating her uncle's evil and aspirations. But then, she took comfort in knowing that he had underestimated hers. 'Getting out of here' was not her style.

It took her just half a second to blow the Leech into a thousand pieces. Jingles shrieked as she was completely covered in the bloodied mess. Violet turned and shot two of the Nuns at point blank range, cutting them down before they could react. The third turned to her with its eyes blazing red and fired, hitting her directly in the centre of the chest. Violet catapulted backwards from the impact, hitting the floor hard and laying shocked, unsure as to how she had survived. Yet apart from what felt like bruising, she was still very much alive.

Rolling over, she lifted her arm and blew the third Nun up, sparks and pieces of circuitry raining down.

A warm hand grasped her shoulder. Ready to fight, she looked up only to see Camdex peering down at her.

'Thank goodness you ate your cheese!'

Surprised and confused, Violet could see a huge gaping hole at the back of the room, and through it streamed the Sisters of the Living. Aware of their presence, the Sisters of the Dead turned as one, their eyes lighting up in anticipation of an attack. But the Sisters of the Living had their own defences. Those in the front line raised their arms and blasts of red shot out from their palms, their weaponry just like Violet's.

The Sisters of the Dead shot rays from their eyes in counter attack, and the fighting began.

The hole in the wall was now encircled with a swirling mist. The Sisters of the Living continued to pour through, but these new Nuns had a surprise for their counterparts. In unison they held their palms to the air and winged objects lifted off. The objects flew across the divide between the fighting sides, and honed in on the evil Nuns, specifically targeting their eyes. As though recoiled on a rubber band, the goggle-like gadgets snapped across the Nuns faces, covering their eyes and instantly adhering to their skin. The Nuns grappled with the goggles, but the bonding between goggle and Nun was inseparable. Camdex had developed them so that on a cellular level the two would become one. As more and more evil Nuns became blinded and unable to shoot, the advantage began to sway towards the Sisters of the Living.

Jingles wasted no time. She turned and fled, disappearing through a side doorway.

Camdex had pulled Violet to the side, joined by Jessica who had apparently appeared from nowhere, although she had actually come in through the hole in the wall behind the Nuns. The three instinctively formed a group ready to face Syntax, who stood purple with fury. Enraged, he threw out his hand, ready to blast them to pieces, but was held back by a protective green barrier from Camdex.

Violet sensed movement above them; three birds had flown in. She quickly realised they were not there to help. The birds were now controlled by Ethan and were heading straight to attack. As their fire power rained down, Violet could only guess as to how long their protection would hold out. She looked to see if any Nuns could assist through the green haze, but instead saw flashes of colour stream past. It was another bird.

'The Symbiosis, Budgie!' Camdex screeched. 'Shoot it!'

Budgie *always* did what his master instructed. Without hesitation, his eyes unleashed their maximum destruction, directed at the star shaped computer. The Symbiosis glowed briefly before exploding, the carefully constructed electronic neurons and circuitry obliterated in a single flash of power. Ethan shuddered and like the old man before him, his body went limp, his sensory input terminated.

The three birds also instantly stopped firing, cut off from their instructions, no longer controlled by good or evil. Their flight became directionless, and they fluttered to the ground, motionless. All except for Budgie, who remained primed for attack. Camdex allowed himself a wry smile. Budgie was never controlled by the Symbiosis; he was completely independent and controlled only by himself. He was, in effect, Camdex's insurance policy in case something went wrong with the other birds. It was always better to be prepared for emergencies with a back-up plan.

Camdex pointed at the black monolith, and Budgie obliged with another blast of destruction. The monolith shattered, and with it ended Syntax's plan of domination. The fighting between the Nuns had now died down; the remaining Sisters of the Dead were blinded and helpless.

Syntax lowered his palm, ceasing the attack on his brother, and the twins took stock of each other. For them, they were now the only people in the room, two brothers so opposite to each other, yet who understood each other perfectly.

'I dedicated my life to stopping you,' Camdex said plainly, pushing the hair from his face which had suddenly sprouted. 'Every second I've been watching you, knowing what you are capable of, ready to oppose anything that you construct or invent. All those years ago, when you created the Sisters of the Dead with their solar panel teeth, I created the Sisters of the Living, an improved version who charge themselves with kinetic motion! But I had to do better, to provide further protection for when you made your move. I created the Symbiosis and birds to get a head start, to get control before you did, and to make our society function once more. And I even knew the girls were not safe with you. I fed them cheese impregnated with micro filaments, harmless to them but which would absorb the energy from the Nun's firepower if ever they were attacked; firepower which you copied off me when I was dabbling in weaponry. I've *always* had to be one step ahead!'

'You didn't know I built my own Symbiosis,' Syntax sneered. 'How did you find it here?'

'Ethan's detective Jess knew where he was because he was wearing her wrist-o-gram. She found out your connections with the Deliverance after investigating Rose and Violet, and then contacted me. She's very smart, you know.'

Jess looked pleased at the compliment.

'It's not over,' Syntax said bluntly.

Camdex grunted and changed the topic. 'You look quite stupid with that extra brain. And it didn't help. Even if you are more intelligent now, it turned out to be your weakness. You see, the trouble with really intelligent people, is that they underestimate everybody else. You thought you were so superior, it didn't occur to you that I could actually stop you.' Camdex's voice hardened. 'And I'll always be there to stop you, brother.'

Syntax glared and activated a ring on his finger. 'Will you?'

He gave a sickening smile, as metal strands began extending from his hand, working their way up his body. Within a few seconds he was completely covered, and then he vanished, his smile somehow lingering in the air for a fraction longer.

Camdex stared at the empty space, his face disappearing under his growing hair like a theatrical curtain falling at the end of a play.

225

CHAPTER 20

Side by side, Rose and Mistix lay in their hospital beds. Kredax, Ethan, Jessica and Violet hovered around them. Violet had a scarf coiled tightly around her neck, while Kredax and Ethan had their collars elevated and secured at the front to hide their branded hearts.

The group were astounded at Rose's and Mistix's remarkable survival. When Ethan and Violet had disappeared under the influence of the space chip, Rose had continued to fall, hurtling to the ground unhindered. Her saving grace were her legs; so much stronger than normal thanks to Camdex's technology. She'd landed upright, fracturing almost every circuit and bio-similar reinforced fibre within their structure, but nonetheless saving her. She survived, her legs destroyed, and her broken body discovered by hospital staff at the base of the mountain. She now had to recover enough to prepare for another transplant under the watchful care of her father.

Mistix had also endured a near miss that almost cost him his life. Fighting off the Deliverance, he was badly injured but managed to activate the last remaining pod to escape, transporting it directly to the foyer of the hospital. After undergoing treatment for wounds to his chest and arms, he too was in the process of recovery, and now apparently had to endure the company of those around him, including his brother.

Kredax had escaped unscathed. After becoming

separated from the girls during the Leech attack, he'd returned home, eventually getting in contact with Mistix once he'd returned to the hospital, although only because Mistix had decided to allow it.

Ethan was now returned to being 'good'. Camdex re-activated his inhibitor before he had even become fully conscious after becoming part of the Symbiosis. Ironically, he was quizzing the girls about their persuasions, having decided that neither was evil.

'You could have told me. It never occurred to me that you were… both the same.'

'We especially didn't want *him* to know.' Violet indicated Mistix. 'He could've seen us as a threat and made our job harder.'

'Your job?'

'To protect you.'

Ethan nodded sullenly. 'Because Camdex asked you to look after me?'

'Yes,' Violet affirmed. 'When he realised who you were, he sent me a message directly to my arm. It transmits and interprets the signal and sends a telepathic message to my brain.'

Ethan was impressed, before unease settled on him.

'Did you know what your uncle was doing?'

Violet shook her head. 'We suspected something was happening, but we didn't know what or the extent of what he'd planned. After the Leeches first attacked, we had to find out. We knew Uncle had a connection with the Nuns, but never realised before that he actually made them. He manufactures and stores them at the back of the convent. We were investigating when you appeared.' Violet shivered. 'He's got hundreds there, just waiting to be activated.'

'So that's why Camdex made the Sisters of the Living. In case they ever came alive and attacked.'

Violet nodded.

'But why lie about being twins?' He could tell it was a sore point for both the girls.

'You don't understand, Ethan,' Rose said softly, obviously weakened after her injuries. 'Our twins attacked us; that's how I lost my legs and Violet her arm. There was a fire and even though…' she swallowed hard, '…they did what they did, we tried to save them, but we were too badly hurt. When they died, half of *ourselves* died that day. To lose a twin destroyed us. But then, when Violet and I realised that we looked so similar and are of a similar age, we knew we could fill a gap in each other's lives. Our bond is as strong as two twins could ever be.' They reached for each other, their hands clasping.

'But you turned off the wrist-o-gram so Jess couldn't contact me.'

Rose looked ashamed. 'I'm sorry. That *was* me. When she mentioned our shoes, I knew she knew we weren't twins. If *we* feel like we are twins then let us *be*, it's not anybody else's business! And there were so many rumours when our sisters and Mum died that Violet and I had killed them.' Rose's eyes filled with tears. 'I didn't want to go through all that again. Their death was their own fault. It wasn't ours!'

Ethan nodded. 'So how could your father build that… Symbiosis? To hold someone prisoner like that in *that* state?'

Violet was defensive when she spoke. 'It was the only way! With a purely technological computer there would always be the chance of information corruption. Even with the most advanced protections, hacking technology is also so advanced that it could never be totally secure. There *had* to be a biological element to it which could never be attacked remotely without knowing his genetic coding.'

'The birds did attack people though even before Ethan was connected to the Symbiosis,' Kredax pointed out. 'And the food trolleys.'

Violet nodded. 'The Symbiosis' prime directive was to always act in a way considered to be good. Uncle was able to introduce a new wave pattern which changed the definition slightly, to that of being 'fair'. So, the computer rationalised that because good people had been in control for so long, it was now fair that bad people had a chance to be in control. The birds were only affected temporarily before the Biological Insertion fixed the problem, which is exactly one of the reasons why he needed to be there! The orders for the birds to kill also affected the trolleys' electronics.'

'The Biological Insertion is the old man?' Kredax asked.

Violet nodded. 'He doesn't suffer. He only knows his life inside the computer.'

'Ethan certainly enjoyed it from what I've heard,' Mistix chuckled, and then coughed as he obviously felt pain from his chest wounds.

Ethan cast his eyes down. 'It was… exhilarating.'

'Why didn't Camdex get help from the Society if he knew his brother was behind everything?'

'Because he is my responsibility,' Camdex muttered, appearing through the door. 'Always was, always will be; best to keep it that way.' He now had his hair back in a pony tail, which had snaked itself down towards ground level.

'Has anyone got any scissors? I need some scissors. Damn hair.'

His request was ignored.

'Where's Uncle now?' Rose asked.

'Who knows?' Camdex grumbled. 'I thought I heard him in the laboratory earlier, but he didn't hang around. I'm sure he'll be using that extra brain of his to think up something else.'

'And Jingles?'

Camdex shrugged. 'She's disappeared.'

'What about the Symbiosis?'

'It's working again, and the birds have destroyed most of the Time Leeches, which is good.'

'You put that man back into the Symbiosis?' Ethan said incredulously.

'He wanted to go back,' Camdex explained. 'It's all he's ever known.'

Ethan shook his head, the explanation disagreeable. 'The Society should know about Syntax,' he said, a trace of anger in his voice.

'No, no, no,' Camdex said resolutely. 'I can deal with him. The Society *is* helping to protect the Symbiosis now though, since I repaired it.'

'The Society is probably busy keeping an eye on

somebody else,' Mistix said pointedly. All eyes looked to him.

'Turns out Ethan is just as dangerous as Syntax. Now that I'm off the case of protecting him they are sure to get involved.'

Ethan flushed. 'The inhibitor is back on. I'm not dangerous.'

Mistix raised an eyebrow. 'Aren't you? I realised something wasn't right with you when you came up on my holographic map as a Snake-shift.'

Ethan opened his mouth to answer, but then chose to ignore him, instead looking at Camdex, his eyes flashing.

'You put that space chip in me. Why did you put it in those other people, the others who disappeared?'

Camdex shook his head. 'I didn't do that. I don't know why they had them. I'm not even sure that Syntax activated them.'

'Then why don't you put the inhibitor chip in everyone? Make everyone… change.' Ethan was accusing.

'Force half the population to change? There are ethical considerations.'

Ethan's hands clenched. 'You forced it on *me*!'

'I had to balance the risk for society of not doing it. It wasn't an easy choice, no, definitely not. The Symbiosis wasn't an easy choice either. But it worked! Society was stabilised.'

Ethan pursed his lips, his brain swirling with questions. 'I want to know everything that you did to me when I was younger. What *am* I?' He paused. 'And why are they called Time Leeches? Why *Time*?'

Camdex cleared his throat. 'Well, yes. That might be a good idea. Perhaps we can go to my laboratory and discuss it. Do you like cheese?' Camdex turned to go. 'Come with me, I can tell you everything.' He cleared his throat, and then added, 'I have biscuits too.'

Almost reluctantly, Ethan went to follow, but then pointedly looked at Mistix. His eyes were dark.

'You deliberately tried to turn me against Rose and Violet. I think, just to entertain yourself. You did everything you could to show me that even though you were protecting me, you were still basically not on our side.' Ethan's lips pursed. 'But I don't believe you. You saved me from the Deliverance and almost died trying. You nearly sacrificed yourself for me. So, when you say people can't change, you are wrong. People can choose to be who they want to be, and you proved it.' Ethan made his point and left.

And for once, Mistix had nothing to say.

Jess turned to the remaining group. 'Well, that all seems wrapped up for the moment; just one more thing to sort out.' She looked meaningfully at Kredax. It took him a second to realise.

'I need to be paid, dear.'

Kredax nodded furiously. 'Of course, Jess. Of course! Let's sort it out now.'

He looked down at the diminutive lady with purple hair. By all accounts from what the others had told him, her investigations had quite literally saved the day. Whatever she wanted in payment, it was a small price to pay for her help. Jess held up her wrist-o-gram, and keyed in some data. Kredax held up his hand with a transactional ring, and the funds were transferred immediately.

Jess smiled, satisfied. 'Until next time, dears. May your twins...' she looked pointedly at the girls, 'Or those you choose to *be* your twin, be with you *always*.'

Kredax smiled inquisitively. 'What do you mean next time? Will there be a next time?'

Jessica turned, walking away. 'Oh yes. I would say so,' she said mysteriously. 'Most definitely.'

Smiling, she disappeared out the door, but not before leaving everyone agog at the uncovered, gigantic, right-side-up heart fully exposed on the back of her neck, proudly displayed as an example to all.

www.ingramcontent.com/pod-product-compliance
Lightning Source LLC
Chambersburg PA
CBHW070013120726
47909CB00003B/908